BUNNIES IN THE BATHROOM

'I want Button and Barney to come to *my* home,' John declared.

'*You* want them?' Mandy repeated.

'Yes, why not? I know a lot of stuff about rabbits now. I went straight in and asked the woman in the shop to keep them to one side for me. Come on, you two! Let's go home and tell Dad.'

'But . . . !' Mandy felt a niggling doubt rise to the surface. What would happen to Button and Barney when John was away at school?

John ran ahead. 'I bought them with my own money! Button and Barney are going to be all mine. It's going to be great!'

Mandy and James followed him up the lane. Mandy kept her fingers crossed, but she had a nasty feeling that it wouldn't be quite that simple. How would John feel when he had to leave the rabbits behind? And who would be left to take good care of Button and Barney?

Animal Ark series

1 Kittens in the Kitchen
2 Pony in the Porch
3 Puppies in the Pantry
4 Goat in the Garden
5 Hedgehogs in the Hall
6 Badger in the Basement
7 Cub in the Cupboard
8 Piglet in a Playpen
9 Owl in the Office
10 Lamb in the Laundry
11 Bunnies in the Bathroom
12 Donkey on the Doorstep
13 Hamster in a Hamper
14 Goose on the Loose
15 Calf in the Cottage
16 Koalas in a Crisis
17 Wombat in the Wild
18 Roo on the Rock
19 Squirrels in the School
20 Guinea-pig in the Garage
21 Fawn in the Forest
22 Shetland in the Shed
23 Swan in the Swim
24 Lion at the Lake
25 Elephants in the East
26 Monkeys on the Mountain

Sheepdog in the Snow
Kitten in the Cold

LUCY DANIELS

Bunnies
—in the—
Bathroom

Illustrations by Shelagh McNicholas

*Hodder
Children's
Books*

a division of Hodder Headline plc

Special thanks to Jenny Oldfield, and to C. J. Hall, B.Vet.Med.,
M.R.C.V.S., for reviewing the veterinary information contained in
this book

A Catalogue record for this book is available from the British Library

ISBN 0 340 70914 6

Typeset by Avon Dataset Ltd, Bidford-on-Avon B50 4JH

Printed and bound in Great Britain by
Clays Ltd, St Ives plc

Hodder Children's Books
a division of Hodder Headline plc
338 Euston Road
London NW1 3BH

One

'James, come and look at these!' Mandy Hope hovered over a counter full of chocolate bunnies, all wrapped in cellophane and tied up with pink, yellow and blue ribbons. Rows of little rabbits crouched, looking up at her with their enormous almond-shaped eyes. Their ears seemed to twitch. 'They're so lifelike!' she whispered.

James Hunter sighed. 'Uh-oh, I can see this is going to be your newest craze. Rabbits!'

'What's wrong with that?' Mandy knew he was teasing. 'It's nearly Easter, isn't it? Easter bunnies!'

'Yes, well, they're better than boring old eggs, I

suppose,' James grumbled. He joined Mandy at the counter. There were rows of fat chocolate pigs beside the shy bunnies, and some cheerful frogs squatting, dark brown and shiny, along the back of the counter.

'Yes, please?' Mr Cecil said, coming out from the back room. He brought with him the delicious bittersweet smell of melted chocolate. He wore a spotless white coat and sparkling, silver-rimmed spectacles. His head was round and bald and shiny. 'Can I help?'

Mandy took ages to decide. She wanted a small gift for each of her friends in Welford village: for Jean Knox who worked as the receptionist at Animal Ark; for Simon, their nurse; for Lydia Fawcett on the goat farm up at High Cross; and for Ernie Bell in the cottages behind the Fox and Goose pub.

'Do you do squirrels?' she asked Mr Cecil. A squirrel would be ideal for Ernie, who had his own pet squirrel in a run in his back garden.

'Squirrels? Certainly.' The old man spread his hands to display the bushy-tailed creatures. Each clutched a hazelnut in its front paws. 'In dark chocolate, milk chocolate, or white chocolate?' he asked.

Mandy hesitated again. 'Oh!' she sighed. 'They're all so . . . perfect!'

'Frogs for me,' James decided in an instant. He pointed to the comical shapes, all squatting on their haunches, their mouths stretched wide. He ordered six in milk chocolate and waited for Mr Cecil to pack them into a white cardboard box with 'Cecil's Confectionery' printed in elegant silver letters on the top and sides.

'Of course, they'd be too good to eat.' Mandy switched her gaze back to the baby rabbits. She peered once more through the glass counter and took a deep breath. 'I'll take a squirrel for Ernie, please, a pig for Simon, a frog for Jean, oh – and a bunny for Lydia!' She'd made up her mind at last.

'She'll love you for that!' James warned with a wry grin.

'Why?'

'Her fields are overrun with them. She's always going on about it. Rabbits make such a mess of the land.'

'But Lydia likes them all the same.' Mandy smiled across at her best friend. He looked so serious sometimes, with his glasses and his floppy fringe of dark brown hair. She turned to the shopkeeper. 'I don't suppose you do goats, by any chance?' she said suddenly.

Mr Cecil smiled and his eyes twinkled. 'No, I'm sorry. Their legs are too thin; they'd break. The same with horses, I'm afraid. Now, did you want this little chap in dark, milk, or white?' He pointed to the row of enchanting bunnies.

At last, the big decisions were made and all Mandy's little chocolate animals were safely packed inside a second cardboard box. Then the kind old man smiled and gestured for them to wait. 'I think you'd like to take a peek at something I've just finished,' he whispered. 'And I must say I'm rather pleased with it myself!'

Mandy balanced her light box with both hands and waited for him to return. He came back through the swing-doors, proudly displaying his latest masterpiece. It sat on an icing-sugar nest on a silver cardboard disc about thirty centimetres wide; a huge, glossy, chocolate hen, perfect in every detail, down to her beady eye and last wing feather. When Mandy looked more closely, she saw tiny white chocolate chicks peering out of the nest, and when Mr Cecil lifted the broody hen, there were the discarded shells and three more chocolate eggs with a pale brown sugar coating,

speckled and looking as though they were about to hatch.

'Wow!' Even James allowed himself to be impressed.

Mandy was speechless. Her eyes darted over the beautiful, delicious object.

'Special order,' Mr Cecil said proudly. 'For Mrs Parker Smythe. It's an Easter gift for her little girl, Imogen.'

'Lucky thing!' Mandy breathed. She secretly thought that spoilt Imogen Parker Smythe, who lived in luxury up at Beacon House, just above Welford village, had done nothing to deserve such a special gift. She was a girl who had everything but seemed pleased with none of it.

Mr Cecil glanced across at Mandy. 'You like animals?' He nodded and smiled as she pored over the hen and her brood.

'Ha!' James laughed. 'You could say that!'

'I live at Animal Ark,' Mandy explained. 'My mum and dad are the Welford vets.'

'Ah!' The old man looked up as the doorbell gave a high, tuneful tinkle. Another customer had come into the shop. 'In that case, you'd be interested in the new pet shop that's just opened down the road.'

No sooner said than Mandy shot out on to the street, ahead of James, gabbling her thanks as she went.

James followed. 'Mandy, we have to catch the bus, remember!' He called after her. 'I promised my mum I'd be back home for tea.'

Mandy ran as fast as the precious box allowed her to, down Walton's main street with its rows of smart shop fronts, its cafés and bookshops. 'Just two minutes!' she shouted. 'I think we can still make it!'

She spotted the new pet shop and dashed over to peer through the window. At first she saw only her own reflection; a tall, slim figure in jeans and a sweater, with shortish blonde hair. Then, she made out racks of dog leads, furry playthings for kittens, imitation bones for dogs to chew, packs of dry rabbit food, budgerigar cages, and, at the back of the dark shop, a big glass aquarium with fish darting back and forth; vivid streaks of silver, blue and fiery red.

'Here comes the bus!' James warned.

'Hang on a sec!' The pet shop owner was carrying a bulky cage towards the window, coming out of the gloom of a back room. Struggling, he reached over a ledge and set it firmly in a space in the crowded window, in full view. The cage was lined with fresh straw. There was a clear drinking bottle tilted towards the floor, and when the cage was firmly settled and the warmth of the late sun struck through the glass of the shop window, Mandy saw a small movement. 'Look!' she whispered.

James instantly forgot all about the approaching bus. 'What is it?' He craned forward to look.

Two noses emerged from the more private wooden section, through a hole in the side. They were small, round and brown, with long whiskers. Then the ears came into view, erect and twitching; listening, listening.

'Baby rabbits!' Mandy breathed.

Two small, furry shapes shyly hopped into view. One sat and scratched his ears with his back leg, the other perched upright, his nose twitching. Then he came to the water bottle and began to drink, ears back, eyes still wide and staring.

'They're so perfect!' James marvelled at the tiny creatures. The second baby came to crouch in the sun, side by side, fawn-coloured and adorable, with great, liquid, dark eyes. 'But you've got three rabbits at home,' he reminded her. 'So don't get any ideas.' He glanced up at the name of the new shop; 'Pets' Parlour', written in bright red and gold letters.

'But *you* haven't!' Mandy turned sideways and widened her blue eyes in his direction. 'James . . .'

'No!' He jumped in quickly. 'Blackie and Eric are already a handful!' But he sighed all the same. The baby rabbits were irresistible. Still, Blackie, his Labrador, needed a lot of walking to keep his weight down, and Eric the kitten was into everything.

'Do you think someone nice will come along and buy them?' she asked with a touch of regret. She yearned to take them home, yet she knew that common sense said no. Animal Ark was always overflowing with visitors and patients; anything from Jack Russells with mites in their ears, to badgers wounded in traps.

'They're bound to,' James reassured her.

'I just hope they buy both of them together. Rabbits like company.' Slowly she stood back from the shop window. She smiled briefly at the owner; a tall young man in a dark blue sweater, with a red checked shirt.

'Mandy!' James reminded her about the time. He heard the bus engine choke and roar at the stop on the other side of the street.

Mandy stepped back again. 'Bye, bunnies!' she said wistfully. The two babies took slow, identical, rocking hops across their cage and sat, ears up, noses twitching.

'Don't worry, they'll find a good home,' James said as they crossed the busy street. They climbed on to the bus just as the driver let off the handbrake and signalled to pull out. He took their money and they sank into a nearby seat.

As the bus drew out of town and set off over the moor road towards Welford, Mandy found herself dreaming. Spring was in the air. The sticky-buds on the horse chestnut trees were beginning to burst open, the hawthorn hedges were tipped with green. In the fields, lambs nibbled at fresh young shoots or skipped up and down the hillside. She would have called those twin rabbits Barney and Button, she decided, and they would have the best food, with carrots and apples as a treat every weekend. She stared up at the drifting clouds as the bus rocked and swayed along the twisting road.

Gently James dug his elbow against her arm. 'Look!' He pointed out of the window.

The sun had sunk low, leaving the crest of the eastern hill bathed in warm, yellow light. Shadows fell long and deep over the rough pasture. In the distance there was a stretch of pale purple heather that ran all along the valley ridge. Nearby, in the soft sunlight, the green field was dotted with wild rabbits.

They sat in twos and threes; small brown shapes with pointed ears. At the sound of the bus they stamped their back legs and sniffed the air for danger. They looked startled, froze for a split second, then bolted. They fanned out across the field, scattering into the brambles and ditch bottoms. Some made for their underground runs. They vanished inside with a flash of white tail and one last kick of their powerful hind legs.

'Brilliant!' Mandy said. Then she turned to James. 'You were right!'

'What?' He blushed under her direct gaze.

'Today *is* the day for rabbits!' She held her box of chocolate animals safely on her knee as the bus jolted and lurched.

Two

The bus dropped them off outside the Fox and Goose. Mandy spotted Ernie Bell and his neighbour, Walter Pickard, sitting outside the pub. The two old men were chatting as usual on the porch by the front door of the low stone building. One either side of the door, they sat and watched whoever came and went.

'There you are!' Mandy went across with a bright smile.

'Where else?' Walter asked.

'Like a pair of bookends, we are,' Ernie agreed. 'You always know where to look for us on a fine night like this, sitting over a good pint, putting the world to rights. You can't beat it!' He took a sip from his glass, then pointed to Mandy's box. 'What've you got in there?'

'Aha, close your eyes!' Mandy replied. James joined her, and together they opened the boxes and took out one of the chocolate figures.

'Happy Easter!' they cried. Mandy presented a squirrel to Ernie and James gave a frog to Walter, who kept his eyes closed, his hands outstretched.

They opened their eyes. 'By gum!' Ernie said with a look at the squirrel. 'Lord knows what Sammy will make of this!' He gave Mandy a crooked, embarrassed smile.

'Well, I'll be . . . !' Walter's frog smiled up at him. 'He's a funny little fellow!'

'Don't you like them?' James was anxious not to offend the two old men. Walter was a cat lover; a steady, reliable friend to Mandy and James. Ernie seemed grumpier, with his low, growly voice and short, grey stubble. But adopting Sammy the squirrel and Tiddles the cat had softened him up, and ever since he'd always been willing to help them out of a tight corner.

Ernie sat and studied his cellophane-wrapped squirrel. 'What do I do with him? Eat him, or stick him on my mantelpiece?'

'Nay, the poor chap would melt by the fire!' Walter put in. He grinned at James. 'Young sir, you should never have gone to this trouble for old Ernie and me, you know!'

'Hey, hey, I'm not so old!' Ernie grumbled. He winked at Mandy. 'I reckon you've been into Walton and paid a visit to Harry Cecil's posh shop. He's not cheap, I'm told. You shouldn't have, like Walter says.'

His face set in a frown, but Mandy could tell he was pleased. She and James turned to leave, but Walter half stood up from his bench and stopped them.

'Hang on a minute! What's this?'

A low, dark green car sped down the high street, past the post office. It drew into the pub carpark and the engine died.

'It's the boss!' Ernie said, meaning Mr Hardy, the pub landlord. He called a warning to the bar staff inside. 'Look lively! He's back!'

They heard empty glasses clink and rattle as the staff quickly removed them from view.

'Didn't he go over to fetch his boy earlier this afternoon?' Walter asked. He turned to James. 'It seems to me young John Hardy is in for a surprise when he goes inside!'

John had just got out of his father's car. He looked up at the pub, at the room where he lived with his father during the holidays. During term time he lived seventy or eighty kilometres away at Grange School in the Lake District.

James frowned, then turned to Mandy. 'Didn't his dad tell him about Sara?'

'Shh!' Walter warned.

Mandy widened her eyes and shook her head. John's dad, Julian, had announced his engagement just a week ago. His fiancée was one of the women who helped behind the bar.

'Just look at that whacking great suitcase,' Ernie pointed out. 'What's he got in there, the kitchen sink?'

Mandy saw Mr Hardy lift a case out of the boot. He let it thump heavily to the ground.

It was all too easy to forget about John Hardy when he was away at school. Mandy had known him all her life, yet never known him. That was the peculiar thing. He was eleven, the same age as James, and he was even born in the same week at Walton Maternity Hospital. He was a small, neat, ordinary-looking boy, with dark, wavy hair that seemed to make his face rounder and a bit too goody-goody. It was the sort of hair that always stayed in place. He was never untidy, never hot, never running; always walking in his cool, collected manner. He looked more grown-up than eleven, but Mandy never thought he looked very happy.

'Come on, John,' his father said, leaving the suitcase where it was. He headed for the front door with eager steps. 'Leave that. I've got some news for you, and there's someone inside I want you to meet.' He smiled and went on ahead.

Mandy saw John hesitate. He was wearing a light Aran sweater and jeans. His white sports shoes looked brand-new, but somehow he looked as if he was in his Sunday best. Then Sara came to the door to greet them both. She looked nervous as she stood there waiting.

Ernie grunted, but Walter leaned across and jabbed him with his elbow. 'I'm saying nothing!' Ernie protested. But Mandy thought his sour look said plenty.

They watched uneasily as Sara clasped her hands in front of her.

'John, this is Sara,' Mr Hardy said, his voice tinged with pride and affection. There was a broad smile on his face as he leaned over and gave the woman a reassuring peck on the cheek.

John stood stock-still. He frowned at his father.

'Didn't I say he should have told the boy beforehand?' Ernie mumbled.

'Shh!' Walter warned again. He took a long sip from his glass.

But Mandy agreed with Ernie. If your father suddenly got engaged, you'd want to be the first to know. 'This isn't the kind of Easter surprise I'd like!' she whispered to James. She felt sorry for John, standing there by his suitcase.

'John, this isn't like you,' Mr Hardy said. The smile had vanished from his face.

Instead of saying hello to the fair-haired woman, as his father wanted, John deliberately turned aside and made a great show of having spotted Mandy and James. He greeted them like long-lost friends. 'Hey!' He waved, and strode across. 'Just the people I wanted to see!'

'I don't think!' Ernie muttered.

'John!' Julian Hardy called, obviously annoyed.

'Hello, John,' Mandy stammered. 'How was school?'

'Fine, thanks. I wanted to talk to you about a project I have to do this holiday.' Still he ignored his father and poor Sara, who between them came out and struggled towards the door with the

outsize suitcase. 'This project has to do with animals,' John explained. But his warm tone seemed forced. 'I have to choose an animal and study it in its natural habitat. You know all about animals, don't you, Mandy? You must do; you live at the vets' place.'

Mandy swallowed hard and glanced at James. John Hardy seemed to have the habit of coolly ignoring everyone except the person he wanted to speak to. For the moment, that was her. 'What kind of animal?' she said, blushing at his rudeness.

'That's what I want to talk to you about,' John began. But before he could get any further, his father reached the door. Mr Hardy had to stoop to enter the porch. Mandy noticed that he had the same wavy hair as his son, but a thinner face, and there was a scattering of grey at the temples. He turned to whisper a word to Sara, who nodded, smiled emptily, then went inside once more.

'John!' Mr Hardy said in a stern voice. 'Come here!'

His son pursed his lips. 'I'll come and see you at Animal Ark soon,' he told Mandy. Then he obeyed his father.

'I said it meant trouble!' Ernie warned.

Mandy saw Walter lean over and carefully, deliberately, step on his toe.

'Ouch!' Ernie yelled.

Julian Hardy took John off to a far corner of the carpark to give him a good dressing-down for his rudeness to Sara.

Mandy heard his raised voice. She saw John duck his head and take a step back.

'Well, I'm off home now,' James said quickly, and shot off down the road.

'Bye!' Mandy waved. She didn't like rows either, but somehow she felt rooted to the spot, there outside the Fox and Goose. Soon Mr Hardy lowered his voice and led John out of sight, round the back of the pub. 'Why did John behave like that?' she asked Walter and Ernie.

'Refuse to say hello to Sara, you mean?' Walter shrugged. 'It looks like it was too much to cope with. The poor lad's had his dad to himself all these years.'

'He's not usually like that,' Mandy agreed. Just the opposite. Whenever she'd seen him before, John was always annoyingly polite. 'But he'll soon find out that Sara's OK. I like her. She calls in at Animal Ark sometimes to chat with my mum. She's just moved up to Welford from Sheffield.'

'OK or not, John doesn't want to know,' Ernie pointed out.

'But she even looks great,' Mandy objected. Sara wore fashionable, bright clothes, and looked young for her age. Mandy's mother and Sara had been at school together.

'Give him time!' Walter stood up. 'It'll sort itself out.' He picked up the chocolate frog from the bench beside him and strolled the short distance to his own cottage.

Ernie gave a grimace. 'Maybe.' He followed slowly after Walter. 'Then again, maybe not.'

Mandy stood for a while in the empty porch. *Poor John,* she said to herself. *It can't be easy coming home to find everything has suddenly changed.*

She wasn't surprised when, just seconds later, a side door flew open and John Hardy burst out. His father shouted after him, but the boy took no notice.

He ran through the walled garden at the back of the pub. He flung open the gate and began to leap, then stumble, up the steep hill. He cut across one field, vaulted a low stone wall and kept on running. Mandy had glimpsed his face as he came out. It was crumpled and tear-stained. John looked desperate.

Where can he run to? Mandy wondered. He was bolting, just like a rabbit. She watched him charge wildly up the hill into the middle of nowhere.

Three

'Run, rabbit, run, rabbit, run, run, run.
Here comes the farmer with his gun, gun, gun!'

Mr Hope's rich baritone voice rang out through the empty surgery.

'He'll get by without his rabbit pie,
So run, rabbit, run, rabbit, run, run, run!'

'Very nice,' Jean Knox commented, peering into the treatment room. She had just arrived at Animal Ark. 'Now, where did I put that appointment book?' She searched high and low behind the reception desk. 'I don't know, I'd forget my head if it were loose!'

Mandy grinned at her dad, then went through and put her hands straight on the big red diary lying on the desk. 'Here it is!'

Their grey-haired receptionist gave a surprised gasp. 'Oh, thank you, Mandy dear. What would I do without you?' Jean, flustered as usual, began the search for her car keys. 'Now *where* did I put those keys?' she muttered.

'In your coat pocket?' Mandy suggested.

'Ah yes, how clever!' She felt in her pocket and gave a relieved sigh.

Jean went back to reception, clutching her keys, searching for her glasses, which hung as usual on a chain round her neck.

Mandy giggled. 'Dad, do you need me?' she asked. It was the first proper day of her school holiday, a Monday morning, and she had great plans. She and James wanted to go bird-watching by the river. He'd recently seen a kingfisher wing its way under the low stone arch of the old bridge, and they wanted to spot it together.

'Twitching, is it?' Dad said, locking the door of the drugs cupboard and looking at his watch. 'Twitching' was his name for crouching in the undergrowth with a pair of binoculars, waiting for the kingfisher to show up.

'I've got to feed the rabbits first,' she announced. 'Then maybe we'll go twitching. James said he'd ring me.'

She went out into the garden, armed with the bag of dried oats and other cereal for Flopsy, Mopsy and Cottontail. She thought of scatter-brained Jean, whom she often felt like teasing. 'Now, *where* did I put those rabbits?' she said, teetering on the doorstep.

Dad laughed and wandered out after her. The grass was dewy in the cool morning air as they headed for the hutch at the bottom of the garden.

Mandy greeted her three rabbits and quietly set about clearing the cage of the old bedding, while Dad set first Flopsy, then Mopsy, then Cottontail out in the long wire run where they exercised. Big, sleek, black and white rabbits, they sat in the sun and combed their whiskers.

'Dad, I was wondering. How do you think they'd feel if I changed their names?' she asked. She laid fresh straw in the clean cage. *You grow out of names,* she thought. Now she preferred Button and Barney, and perhaps Benji in honour of James's cat, who had died. The old names seemed a little childish.

'Hmm,' Dad said thoughtfully. 'On the whole, I think they'd probably prefer to stay the same.'

'You're probably right,' she agreed. 'Flopsy, Mopsy and Cottontail is what they've always been.'

Dad helped Mandy by tying a tight knot in the top of the bag of used straw and droppings. 'Good for you,' he said.

She smiled.

'Mandy, you've got a visitor!' Mrs Hope called from inside the house. Her long, red hair was framed in the doorway, and shone bright in the morning sun. 'It's John Hardy!'

'Uh-oh!' Mandy stood up. She'd managed to forget the uncomfortable scene at the Fox and Goose when John had snubbed his father's new fiancée. Now she remembered that he'd promised to call in at Animal Ark.

'Trouble?' Dad asked.

'Not really. I'd better go in and see, though.' She left her father to finish tidying up in the garden and traipsed indoors. Her mum had vanished somewhere upstairs, so she stood face to face with John in the empty kitchen.

'Hello, Mandy,' he said. He was calm and matter-of-fact again, but she still had a clear memory of his tear-stained face as he ran up the hill. He'd come today equipped with camera, notebook and binoculars, and stood looking annoyingly neat and studious. He forgot to smile when he greeted her.

'Hi.' Her own friendly smile faltered. Why did she feel as if she'd just walked into an exam room? Her stomach knotted as she felt him sum up her and her surroundings. She kicked her dad's scruffy slippers out of sight under the table.

'Animals!' John Hardy announced. 'What sort do you suggest?' He looked round the kitchen as if a suitable specimen might suddenly appear.

'Well, there's a lot to choose from at this time of year. If you just look around for something to study, there's—'

'Before you go on, don't say tadpoles, whatever you do!' John interrupted. 'Everyone suggests tadpoles, and they're so boring!'

'Oh, but they're not!' Mandy began. 'Their life cycle is amazing!' Then she stopped. She saw his mind was set against them.

'Anyway, that's kid's stuff,' John said. 'No, I want

to study something that's nice to look at, not disgusting, like tadpoles. Something I can take good pictures of!' He tapped his camera, slung on a strap round his neck. It had levers and lenses and buttons all over the place. This was no seaside holiday camera. 'Well?' John prompted. He stood with his feet wide apart on the Hopes' flagged kitchen floor.

She looked to the beamed ceiling for inspiration, then her gaze swept round the room. There on a shelf on the pine dresser sat her Easter present for Lydia Fawcett, all done up in its bright yellow bow. 'Rabbits!' she said suddenly.

'Rabbits?' John looked suspicious. 'Don't they just sit there and eat lettuce?'

'No, they're brilliant creatures to study. I've been reading up about them. For instance, their warrens are amazing! They meet in big underground chambers, held up with tree roots, with air-conditioning and everything!'

'Air-conditioning?'

'Yes, they build their runs facing away from the wind for warmth, but they connect them up with small runs that open on to the fresh air. Of course, they sleep close together for warmth.'

'How do you know all this?' John was still frowning, but the bit about air-conditioning seemed to have roused his interest. He strode to the window to look out down the lane.

'You won't see any down there,' Mandy explained. 'There are too many trees. And rabbits like high ground. Hillsides, where the wind can carry sound, the ground is dry, and they can smell danger.'

'How do you *know*?' John insisted.

'Like I said, I just sat down last night and read a book,' she confessed, feeling herself go red. She'd taken it down from the shelf in the surgery. 'It's over there on the dresser. I'll ask my dad if you can borrow it, if you like.'

The idea of a textbook also appealed to John, as Mandy guessed it would. He was a boy who liked to study. '*The Private Life of the Rabbit* by R.M. Lockley,' he read out loud as he picked up the heavy volume. 'Have you read it all?'

'No, but it's best to study the rabbits out in the wild before you go in for too much reading. Your project will be much better if you begin with a kind of diary of their habits.' Actually, Mandy was keen to get John Hardy to make up his mind. Then she thought she could take him up to the Celtic cross on the moorside, to one of the High Cross fields. At the same time she would deliver the chocolate bunny to Lydia. 'You know; begin with a chapter called "Rabbit Habits", or something like that!' she said eagerly.

No smile appeared in response, to crack the earnest expression on John's face. 'I suppose you're right. I've got thirty-six exposures on this film. Colour. Fast speed. High definition.' He paused again. 'You're sure rabbits are interesting enough?'

'If you've got enough patience to study them – yes!' Mandy grabbed the present from the shelf. 'I know just the place!' she insisted. 'Ready?'

He nodded, and Mandy called up to her mum. She was anxious to set off. 'Won't be long! I'm just taking John up to High Cross!'

'OK!' Mrs Hope's voice floated downstairs. 'Oh, Mandy, James Hunter phoned while you were busy in the surgery. I said you'd ring him!'

'Thanks. I'll do it when I get back.' She scrambled into her jacket, which hung from a hook on the wall, and dashed out of the house.

At least she'd got John Hardy sorted out with a school project. She breathed in deeply and marched alongside him up the lane.

They trekked by the public footpath across the fields beside Brandon Gill's pig farm. Mandy paused to pick up a stick and give Nelson, the great black and white boar, a quick backscratch. Nelson grunted contentedly and trampled the earth.

John wrinkled his nose. 'I'm glad you suggested rabbits, not pigs,' he said.

Mandy's eyebrows shot up. John Hardy had nearly made a joke. In fact, he seemed to be unwinding as they walked. The wind had even ruffled his hair. There was colour in his cheeks, and his dark eyes had come alive. They darted from hedgerow to bramble thicket, searching for rabbits.

It must be difficult for him, she thought again, *trying to settle in at home, with Sara there so much of the time.* Mandy knew better than to mention Sara's name outright, or to seem too curious. Walter Pickard was right; John would need time to get used to the new situation.

As he relaxed, John began to chat about the Celtic cross landmark way up on the hill, past Beacon House. He knew its history and how it had come to be there. Mandy noticed he didn't vary his pace, but strode on like a man with a mission. Most kids she knew would stop to poke round in ditches or to climb a tempting tree. But John Hardy set his face straight ahead and made it a route march. Soon they'd passed the grand iron gates of Beacon House, the Parker Smythe place, and then the entrance to Upper Welford Hall. Mandy had to drag John to a halt by the old five-barred gate that marked the entrance to High Cross Farm.

'Hang on a sec!' she gasped. 'We're here! Let me just pop in and ask Lydia if we can use her fields to scout around for rabbits. And I want to give her this.' She held up the cellophane package.

'Hmm . . .' John frowned. 'I'll wait here and keep a lookout!' He stood bolt upright, binoculars poised.

Mandy dashed inside. She found Lydia in the barn, tending to her beloved goats. Dressed in her oldest wellingtons and her tattered brown work jacket, she was mucking out the stalls and turning each of her goats out to graze in the spring pasture. Houdini, the most mischievous of all, stood in his stall and snickered at Mandy as she approached.

'Hello, Houdini!' Mandy circled her arms about his neck and hugged him. Houdini bared his teeth. His hooves clattered against the wooden door. 'Steady, boy!' She backed off and greeted Lydia. 'Happy Easter!' she said shyly, handing over the small present.

'What's this?' A smile lit up Lydia's face, so that it wrinkled like a shiny old apple. 'Why it's a little bunny rabbit; how clever!' She unwrapped the chocolate like a child at Christmas, then she perched the rabbit gleefully in the palm of her hand.

In an instant, Houdini's bony head darted forward, and he wrapped his rubbery lips round the too-tempting gift. Gulp! Swallow! Lick! It was gone.

'Oh!' Lydia cried out, her face crumpling. Then she laughed. 'Oh, Houdini!'

Mandy joined in the laughter. 'He must have thought it was for him!'

'Tut!' Lydia clicked her tongue. 'His manners are appalling, and he's old enough to know better!' With a good-natured pat of the goat's neck, she unbolted the door and led him out into the farmyard. 'I bet it tasted first class, didn't it, boy?' she grumbled. 'And I'm sure you'd like to say a big thank you to Mandy here!'

Houdini tossed his head and trotted on.

'Talking of rabbits . . .' Mandy said as she spied John Hardy waiting patiently by the gate.

'Were we?' Lydia shot Mandy a quick glance. 'Oh, yes, rabbits . . . chocolate . . . oh, Houdini . . . oh dear!' She chortled and led him on, out to the near pasture. 'Rabbits, yes. Well, we have plenty of them round here, of course.' She let Houdini loose in the field, closed the gate, and leaned forward against the top bar. She gestured towards the field full of fresh dandelions, willowherb and yellow coltsfoot. 'Not in here, of course. The little nuisances know to keep off when the goats are about. No, the sly things keep their distance. But if you go up to the far pasture, the one beyond the house, that field will be alive with them. You can't move up there without tripping over a rabbit hole!'

As Lydia grumbled on, Mandy lost heart. It really did seem that even gentle Lydia saw rabbits as pests. In that case she might not be keen to let a stranger from the village begin his study on one of her fields.

'Mind you, I have to admit that they're bonny little things.' She leaned both elbows on the gate and clasped her broad hands. 'And friendly, so long as you keep your distance; and who can blame them? Many a time I go up there in the evening and watch them come out to feed. They're quite delightful!' She laughed and brought herself up short. 'We farmers aren't supposed to have a soft spot for rabbits, I suppose!'

'But you wouldn't mind if a friend of mine came up to take pictures and make notes, would you?' Mandy seized her chance. 'He has to do some work on rabbits for a school project. I said I thought it would be OK.'

Lydia stood upright and glanced in John's direction. 'That's not young James Hunter, is it?' She screwed up her eyes and raised one hand to shield them from the sun.

'No, it's John Hardy from the Fox and Goose.'

Lydia nodded, then looked up at the sun. 'Time I was getting on with the cheese-making,' she said. 'You know there's no peace for the wicked!' She glanced again at the lonely figure by the gate. 'Tell your friend he's welcome. And to call in at the house for a cup of tea whenever he has the time!'

Mandy thanked her and ran back to John. Soon they were up on Lydia's far pasture and he was crouched down behind the rain-blackened stone wall, camera at the ready. One or two rabbits roamed the far side of the field. He stood up suddenly. They stood stork-still, then vanished down separate holes as he clicked the shutter.

'Missed!' he muttered.

'See!' Mandy told him. 'Didn't I say they were clever? They have fantastic hearing!'

John nodded, then scanned the rough, empty field. 'I'll wait,' he insisted. This time he put his binoculars to his eyes and trained them on the grass.

'It's probably a bit late for rabbits by now,' Mandy said. 'But they do like the sun, so maybe a few will come back for a snack!'

'I'll wait,' he said again, crouching down still as a statue. 'You know, I think your idea about rabbits was good,' he admitted, giving Mandy a brief smile. 'Thanks.' And he settled down to watch.

It was the start of a long, patient campaign by the boy from the pub.

A short time later, Mandy left John to go home and phone James. Then her day was busy. First she went bird-watching. After lunch she helped in the surgery, then she popped into Lilac Cottage to visit her grandparents. But when she cycled back up to High Cross after tea, John Hardy was still there, crouched behind a wall. He hadn't moved all day. All round him, scattered on the grass, lay white sheets of paper.

Mandy left her bike at the main gate and walked across.

'Hush!' he warned. The rabbits were coming out in their hordes as dusk approached. This was their liveliest time of day.

Quietly Mandy crouched beside him. Many of the sheets were covered in tiny writing; scrawled notes about sightings and the position of rabbit burrows. Sometimes John had stopped to sketch a rabbit in fine pencil. She picked up one of these drawings and found it beautifully done. The rabbit's eyes shone like blackcurrants out of its soft, furry face. The ears stood straight, paler on the inside, with black, pointed tips. 'This is good!' Mandy exclaimed. 'I never knew you could draw!'

'You never asked!' John whispered. 'Art is one of my favourite subjects at school. Now quiet, please, or you'll scare them off.'

They watched as more rabbits popped out of their holes, then stopped and sniffed the air. They rocked forwards on to their short front legs and lazily hopped towards a tender shoot of cowslip or dandelion. Their ears twitched and they sniffed the air, but they grazed happily enough. The large male rabbits stayed at the centre of the warren, pushing the smaller yearlings to the outskirts. The young ones had to look out for foxes, weasels, or even the vicious rooks that sat high in the ash trees and cawed.

After a day on duty, John seemed to have learned a lot about studying rabbits. He'd taken off his white sweater, realising that his dark blue T-shirt made him stand out less. He moved smoothly, and didn't jerk when he raised his head above the wall to take more photographs. This time the rabbits' ears still twitched in response, but they carried on feeding, untroubled.

'Well done!' Mandy whispered.

John crouched back down and nodded. 'Thanks. I've had a great time!' He confessed it awkwardly, blushing. The sun had brought up the freckles in his dark skin. 'Now I'd like to find a field with an old warren in it; one that's not used any more. I want to explore how the rabbits make their burrows.'

'How about tomorrow?' Mandy suggested. 'You must be starving hungry. And doesn't your dad need to know where you are?'

Sharply John shook his head. 'He doesn't care.' His voice was flat. Carefully he unscrewed the big lens from his camera and packed it into its case.

'Oh, I'm sure he does!' Mandy began.

But John ignored her. 'So where can I find an *old* warren?' he insisted.

She thought hard. 'Let's go and ask Lydia,' she suggested. She could see that this would be the first of many visits this Easter to High Cross and the rabbit fields. John had taken to her idea better than she expected. What's more, it would keep him busy, and well out of the way of Sara and his dad. No wonder he seemed keen.

'You should be a wildlife artist,' she told him as she helped pack away the sketches. 'I never thought you'd be so interested in animals!'

'You never asked!' he said again.

Mandy stared at him. This time she knew it was a joke. She checked his dark brown eyes; they were sparkling. 'Come on, let's go,' she said. They ran down to the farm together, to a cup of hot tea and Lydia's home-made scones.

Four

'Mandy, James phoned again!' Jean Knox called from the surgery.

Mandy had just got back from High Cross. It was the second week of the Easter holiday; every day the weather grew warmer, the trees greener.

'Or was it John Hardy?' Jean's puzzled voice quavered. 'Oh dear, which one was it?'

Mandy went into reception. She felt flushed from the sun, and tired after the day's explorations. 'It can't have been John,' she exclaimed. 'I just left him outside the Fox and Goose.'

'Oh well, it was James, then,' Jean decided. She

was searching for something in a drawer as usual. 'Now where did I put that—'

'Appointment book?' Mandy broke in.

'Yes, how did you know? . . . Oh, thank you, dear!' Jean smiled brightly. 'Yes, now I come to think of it, it must have been James. He told me he was just back from visiting his aunt and uncle in London, and he wondered if you wanted to play tennis.'

'Great, thanks.' Mandy had dashed back to Animal Ark to do her cleaning chores, but she broke off to pick up the phone and ring her friend. 'Sorry, James, I've just been so busy all day. Did you have a nice couple of days in London?'

'It was OK, thanks. What have you been up to?'

'I've been busy helping on John's school project. We're making a detailed study of the female rabbits now, and their young. John's numbered all the burrows with kittens, and . . .'

'Kittens?'

She heard James's voice sounding confused. 'The baby rabbits. They're called kittens. The females are called does. It says so in this book we've got, *The Private Life of the Rabbit* by R.M. Lockley.'

'Oh.' Now James sounded distant and bored.

'Anyway, we've noticed that most of the litters have five kittens. Some have six. And when the yearlings are strong enough, they move off to form new warrens because the old one gets over-crowded with the new babies. They start all over again on fresh ground.' She rattled on.

'Fancy a game of tennis tonight, then?' James asked in an offhand way.

Mandy thought ahead. She hated to turn him down. After all, he was her best friend, and they always tried to arrange to do things together. 'Oh, James, I'm sorry, I can't! I'm going back over to John's to help him choose some photos for his project. I promised!' Then she hit on an answer. 'How about tomorrow morning?' she asked. 'Meet at my house at about ten? I'll have to dig out my racket from somewhere, and see you then.'

'Fine,' came James's quick reply. 'Bye.' The phone clicked and the line went dead.

Jean nodded her approval. 'Good for you. He rang earlier, but you always seem to be out.'

Mandy sighed. 'I know. Anyway, I must get a move on. I said to John I'd be back at his place by six-thirty!' She swept round the treatment rooms like a whirlwind with her disinfected cloths and hot mop and bucket. In the residential unit at the back of the surgery, she spoke nicely to the Persian cat who'd just been spayed. Then she went out briskly to clean and feed her own rabbits. It was time to go. 'See you later!' she called to whoever was inside the house to hear.

'Don't forget to pop in and see your gran sometime soon,' her dad said. He was sitting with his feet up in the lounge. 'She tells me she hasn't set eyes on you for ages!'

'OK, I'll call in later! Got to dash!' Mandy scrambled free of the house and cycled off up the lane. She was eager to see how John's latest batch of photos had turned out. He'd used his zoom lens to take close-ups of the babies as they emerged from the burrows for the first time. They looked like small fawn balls of spun sugar, with enormous eyes and ears.

She propped her bike against the side wall of the pub and nipped in through the garden. She knocked at the door, then went quickly up the back stairs to John's room. It was a low, old house with thick stone walls and small windows. There was a landing halfway up the stairs with a red and blue stained-glass window which overlooked the garden. The old wooden boards creaked as

she went on upstairs, and the dark corridor to
John's room sloped at an odd angle, like a gangway
on a ferry. She knocked loud and clear on the
old panelled door.

'Come in!' John looked up excitedly as Mandy
opened it. 'The photos have arrived!'

'I can see that!' she laughed. John sat amongst
dozens of colour pictures of the rabbits on the
far pasture at High Cross. They were scattered
across the red carpet, and some were pinned
crookedly to his bedroom walls. More scribbled
notes lay across the desk, and his sketches
decorated the front of the wardrobe, the door

into his bathroom, and even inside the bathroom itself. 'It's worse than *my* room, and that's saying something!' Mandy liked to stick pictures of all her favourite animals on the walls at home, but at least she put them on straight and arranged them neatly. John had simply slapped these on anyhow, and she was surprised because he seemed so tidy in other ways.

'They're the best yet!' he announced. He held up a large, glossy photo to the light and studied it. 'See, I got the angle just right on this one, and the focus is really sharp. The doe is sitting upright at the entrance to the burrow. See, even her whiskers have come out clearly!'

Mandy admired the photos. 'They're really good, John. It's going to be difficult to choose the best.' She knelt down on the floor beside him, but then she glanced at her hands and saw that they needed a wash. 'Hang on, I'll just have to go and wash my hands,' she told him. She went through into the small white bathroom.

'I'll nip down and get us some juice.' John managed to tear himself away from his precious pictures.

Mandy heard the bedroom door open and close. She took her time running the water, soaping her hands and gazing round at John's beautiful sketches of rabbits. His pictures showed their gracefulness; the thing she most loved about them herself. He really was a good artist, she thought. 'Bunnies in the bathroom!' she said to herself with a funny little smile.

She dried her hands. John was taking a long time fetching the drinks. She crossed the bedroom floor, picking her way between the photos. Then she peered out into the long, crooked corridor.

'Hi!' A bright, pleasant voice caught her by surprise.

'Oh, hi!' Mandy recognised the golden hair and neat, slim figure of Julian Hardy's fiancée, Sara. She was dressed in a loose, silky, white shirt and a long blue skirt, with open sandals and bare legs. She wore her long hair swept up casually on top of her head, but strands had escaped and caught in her dangling gold earrings. Her face had tanned in the sun, emphasising her wide, light grey eyes. 'I'm looking for John,' Mandy explained, feeling out of place.

'I saw him go downstairs not long ago.' Sara smiled. 'I'm Sara Lawson. I'm engaged to John's dad.'

'I know.' Mandy saw the diamond engagement

ring on her left hand. She blushed. John really would have to get used to the new situation, like it or not. She thought again that Sara seemed friendly and pretty.

'I'm afraid John and I haven't hit it off yet,' she confessed. She seemed to want to talk to someone. 'Things have been a bit tense since he came back from school. He's out studying those rabbits all the time, or else he just stays in his room and avoids me.' She gave an embarrassed little laugh. 'I don't think he likes me much!'

'Oh, he's never said that!' Mandy protested. She felt her clean palms go hot and sticky again. She didn't fancy being caught up in this problem; it seemed too big for her to do anything about.

'Why, what has he said?' Sara stood facing Mandy in the corridor, a serious look on her face.

'Nothing. He never mentions you.' Mandy had spent hours with John during this last week, while James had been away. They'd braved the wind, rain and sunshine up on the fields at High Cross. She'd crouched behind thick tree trunks with him in the hour before dawn, and returned at dusk to study the rabbits. But he'd never once talked about his family or home.

Sara nodded. 'Exactly. He treats me as if I'm invisible. He seems to think that I'll just vanish, I'm sure he does!' She glanced into his room at the sketches on the walls. 'He's got talent though. You have to say that for him.'

'Yes!' Glad to change the subject, Mandy agreed. 'I think he should be a wildlife artist, or a photographer!'

Raised voices from the garden filtered through the open window. Mandy paused and checked Sara's worried expression. They both recognised another row brewing between Julian Hardy and his son.

'And another thing; just when are you going to tidy up that room of yours?' Mr Hardy demanded. His voice came from the kitchen downstairs. 'It's a complete mess in there. You can't expect Sara or me to go in and tidy up after you, if you leave it in that sort of state!'

There was no reply. Mandy heard a fridge door slam shut.

'John, I'm talking to you! I said, when are you going to clean up all that mess? Scraps of paper and drawings everywhere!'

'It's for my school project.' John sounded slow and sulky. 'I've got to get it finished.'

'But you don't have to clutter the whole place up!' Mr Hardy's voice faded, then John appeared from the kitchen at the foot of the stairs. He began to trail up them, a glass of orange juice in each hand. 'Are you listening to me, or am I just wasting my breath?' His father pursued him into the hallway.

Sara took a deep breath and leaned over the banister. 'Leave him alone now, Julian,' she called out. 'I'm sure he'll tidy up when he's finished his project!'

Mandy felt she could have heard a pin drop. John looked up at Sara with a blank expression. Julian stood, taken aback, hands on hips, one foot on the bottom step.

'And you should see his sketches of those rabbits! They're brilliant!' Sara tried to smooth things out.

There was another tense silence. Then John snapped. His face crumpled. 'Who asked you?' he demanded. 'Who said you could go in my room and snoop around?'

Suddenly he turned and tripped. Mandy watched as the two full glasses tipped against the white wall. The orange liquid splashed against it and trickled down. John stared at it in dismay.

'John!' His father yelled out a warning, but it was too late.

Sara put one hand over her mouth and stepped quickly back.

But John dived downstairs with a weird cry. He rushed past his father and fled, head down, straight out through the kitchen, across the garden into the main street. Mandy raced after him.

'Nay,' Ernie Bell advised. He stopped her short by putting out a hand from his position on the bench in the front porch. 'Leave him be. There's enough trouble round here as it is. Don't you go adding to it.'

Mandy glanced down at Ernie, her eyes watering, her heart pounding. She saw John disappear over a stile into the fields behind the McFarlanes' post office.

Ernie was right; she was out of her depth. Sadly she went home in the fading light.

John came over to Animal Ark early next morning. He was dressed in a green zip-up jacket, camera at the ready. His face gave nothing away as Mandy went to answer the door. 'Hi, I thought we could get the bus over to Walton today, before we go up to High Cross.' He waited for her to collect her thoughts. 'There's a book I want to get from the library.'

Mandy glanced at her watch. It was half-past nine. Mrs Hope and Simon were busy in the surgery. Her father was out on his rounds. There was no chance of a lift into town, and she knew that John didn't have a bike. 'I'll just ask Jean what time the next bus goes,' she told him. 'Hang on here a minute.'

Though he looked the same as usual, spruced up and calm, Mandy thought he sounded tense, and she spotted a pleading look behind his eyes, as if he needed her company today of all days. She opened the door into reception, to a chorus of growls, barks and miaows. 'Jean, when's the next bus into Walton?' She leaned across the counter and shouted over the noise.

Jean checked her watch. 'In ten minutes. From the post office.'

'We'll just make it. Thanks!' Mandy made as if to sprint off.

'Mandy!' Jean called.

'See you later. Tell Mum I've gone into town, will you, please?' She shot off back into the house, to find John answering the front door to James Hunter.

James stood on the doorstep, tennis bag in one hand. He wore his blue and red track suit and white tennis shoes. He looked up at John. 'Is Mandy in?' he stammered.

'James!' she gasped. She dashed up from behind. 'Oh no, I forgot!' Both boys stared at her. 'I mean, I didn't exactly forget! Anyway, you're early!' She felt her stomach tilt. What should she do now?

'It's all right, never mind.' James stood there, two steps down in the breezy morning air. 'I should have rung you up to check it was still OK.' He stopped, lost for words.

John stood in the hall with a slight frown creasing his smooth forehead. Then he caught sight of Jean Knox, following Mandy through from the surgery.

'James, can we just change our plan a bit?' Mandy asked. She felt flustered. 'Why don't we all slip over to town together, then fit in a game of tennis?'

'No thanks. I'd rather go on down to the tennis-courts by myself,' James said quietly. He turned and wandered off up the drive. 'I'll find someone to play with, no problem. See you later.'

John blinked at Mandy. 'Is it my fault?' he asked.

'No, of course not; it's not your fault.' Mandy's stomach still hadn't regained its balance. She felt churned up inside.

'Mandy?' Jean said quietly. She came up close. 'John, why don't you go ahead to the bus stop?' she suggested in a firm but kindly voice. 'And perhaps Mandy will join you later.'

A blush flooded across John's face, but he nodded and went off nonetheless. Jean closed the door after him and put an arm around Mandy's shoulder. Then she led her into the kitchen.

'I never meant to do that to James!' Mandy said. She felt helpless, and a kind of hot guilt was creeping up her neck. She put up her hand to hide it.

'No, I'm sure you didn't.' Jean put on the kettle. She seemed to know exactly where everything was at this moment; the switch, the tea-bags, her glasses. She sounded calm and looked gently at Mandy. 'But if you were James and thought that someone had come along and stepped into your shoes, how do you think you would feel?'

'Lousy,' Mandy admitted. 'But it won't be for long. John has to go back to school next week, and he has to finish that rabbit project. I'm just lending a hand!'

'Yes.' Jean gazed steadily at her. 'You know, it puts me in mind of something that happened to me when I was eight; and that's well over fifty years ago now!' She settled at the table opposite Mandy and seemed to look down a long corridor into the past. 'It was summer, I remember, and I'd been on holiday to Blackpool. I brought a stick of pink rock back for my best friend. She was called Margaret; Margaret Taylor. We were like two peas in a pod.

'Well, I went up to her back garden with the stick of rock the minute we got home. She was playing there with a girl who lived down the street; Susan Turnbull. A girl with beautiful blonde plaits. Margaret looked at me across her garden fence. Her nose went up in the air. "I don't want your smelly stick of rock!" she told me. And she turned back to play with Susan. Well, sometimes we can all be nasty and spiteful like that, I know, but it was worse than any smack or telling off I'd had in my entire life, I can tell you.'

'And you were best friends?' Mandy asked. Her throat felt dry and narrow. Did it look as if she'd just done something similar to James?

'Yes. That's probably what put me in mind of you and James.' Jean stopped to sip her tea.

'And did you ever play with her again after that?' Mandy hoped the story would have a happy ending.

'I expect so. Yes, of course I did. Next day she was my best friend again, no doubt. And I suppose we were even nasty to Susan Turnbull on occasions. She was a big-headed girl because her father owned a chemists' shop and drove a Morris Oxford; a big black car,' Jean explained. Then she sighed. 'But I never forgot that stick of rock!'

Mandy jumped up from the table, her mind made up. 'Thanks, Jean!' she said.

'Why, where are you going?'

'To find my tennis racket!' Mandy said.

'It's under the counter in the surgery,' Jean told her with a smile. 'I noticed it lurking there yesterday. And there's a new set of balls and your tennis shoes. I expect your track suit's up in your wardrobe drawer!'

Mandy nearly dropped through the floor with shock. She stared at Jean. 'Thanks!' she stammered again.

'Now, *where* did I put my glasses?' Jean

mumbled. She carried the empty mugs to the sink. 'I'm sure I put them somewhere sensible . . .'

'Round your neck!' Mandy yelled. She was through the door, racket in hand, shoes hooked by their laces round her own neck. She dashed up the drive. 'See you later, Jean!'

James beat her seven-five, six-four, even though she was trying really hard to win.

After the game, they went straight back to Mandy's house for a sandwich lunch.

'Sorry about this morning,' Mandy mumbled, her mouth full of crusty french bread. 'It's just that I was pretty worried about John. Things aren't any better for him at home. In fact, I think they're worse. He can't seem to get over the shock of his dad getting engaged.' She told James about her visit the previous evening.

'Maybe he's jealous?' James said thoughtfully. 'Of Sara, I mean.'

'But she's really nice. He hasn't even given her a chance!'

'You don't when you're jealous, do you?'

Mandy stopped chewing and sighed. 'You're right. Anyway, I am sorry!' she repeated.

James grinned and switched the subject back to tennis. 'You lost it in the vital seventh game of the second set!' he reminded her. 'You served those two double faults.'

She nodded. 'I know, I know; I lost concentration.'

The sound of footsteps on the drive interrupted them. Through the window they could see John Hardy come bounding up to the door. They dashed out, glad to see him looking flushed and excited for once.

'What's got into you?' James demanded. He dragged John inside. 'Did you finish your project?'

John sank breathlessly into a chair. He ran a hand through his wavy hair. 'No, it's not that. I've just got back from town, and guess what?'

'What?' Mandy pushed a drink of juice across the table in his direction.

'There's a new pet shop that's just opened up on the High Street!'

'We know. Pets' Parlour,' James cut in.

'That's the one. But guess what, guess what!' John was almost spluttering with excitement. He unzipped his jacket and rested on the two back legs of his chair. 'They've got rabbits! Rabbits in the window! Little brown ones! For sale!

They're selling pet rabbits!'

'That's Button and Barney,' Mandy grinned. 'Anyway, that's what we call them.' She glanced across at James.

'You mean you've already seen them?' He looked astonished that his news wasn't new.

She nodded. 'Last week. I suppose that means that no one's come along and bought them yet.'

'Yes, thank heavens!' John gasped.

'Why, what are you up to now? Don't you want them to go to a good home then?' She glanced across again at James. What was going on in John's mind?

'No, I want them to come to *my* home!' he declared. He laughed out loud at their surprise.

'*You* want them?' she repeated.

'Yes, why not? I know lots of stuff about rabbits now. I can look after them. I went straight in and paid the money and asked the woman in the shop to keep them to one side for me!' John's face had come alive. He leapt up from his chair. 'Come on, you two! Let's go home and tell Dad!'

'But . . . !' Mandy felt a niggling doubt rise to the surface. What would happen to Button and Barney when John was away at school?

'Come on, what are you waiting for? Come and help me explain to my dad!'

Mandy shrugged, James nodded. 'You seem to have made up your own mind already!' he said.

'You bet!' John ran ahead. 'I bought them with my own money! Button and Barney are going to be all mine! I'll build a hutch, they can live in the garden! This is going to be great!'

Mandy and James followed him up the lane. She kept her fingers crossed for John as they headed for the Fox and Goose, but she had a nasty feeling that it wouldn't be quite that simple. Keeping pets when you had to go away to school was complicated. How would John feel when he had to leave them behind and set off for the Lake District? And who would be left to take good care of Button and Barney?

Five

'Don't be daft, John!' Julian Hardy stood in the kitchen at the back of the pub, armed with two massive plates of ham sandwiches. 'How can we keep pet rabbits here? Where on earth would we put them, for a start?' He was on his way back into the bar to cope with the busy lunch-time rush.

'In the garden, in a hutch.' John's eager face began to shut down. He glanced at Mandy and James, who hung back outside. 'They wouldn't be any trouble, honest!'

'And what happens when you're away at school? Who would you get to feed them then?' Mr Hardy pushed open the inner door with his foot. He balanced the plates carefully. '*And* keep them clean? *And* make sure they got some exercise?' He waited a second for John to see sense.

Mandy sighed. She'd feared this was going to happen.

'But, Dad, it doesn't take long. They're dead easy to look after. Aren't they, Mandy?'

She nodded, but she could see they were fighting a losing battle. Button and Barney would have to spend more time in the pet shop until another kindly owner came along.

'See – Mandy knows! And I've already paid for them, Dad. I can't back out now!'

Mandy looked at James. She could tell that his heart had sunk as low as hers. John was in for another big disappointment.

'Look, can we talk about this some other time?' Mr Hardy was beginning to frown. He hopped and wobbled on one foot, struggling to keep his balance. Then Sara opened the door from the far side. She stopped short, immediately sensing that something was wrong.

'I need to know straight away!' John persisted. 'Rabbits are my main project for science this year. I'll be at home for the whole of the summer to look after them. And I can come back for more weekends and half-terms. You'll hardly have to do anything!'

'That's what you say now, and it's all very well. But just you wait; it'd be me looking after them most of the time. I'd bet a lot of money on it!'

'Honestly, Dad! Listen, they're fantastic, aren't they, Mandy? They're brown all over and really friendly. They need a good home; they're getting bored cooped up in the pet shop all day long. I want to look after them!'

Mr Hardy sighed. 'Listen, once and for all, John. I said no! It's not practical. So you'll just have to go straight back to the shop, tell them you changed your mind, and get your money back!' He marched on through the door. It was his final word.

Sara hovered nervously, just inside the kitchen door. She peered into John's face. 'Never mind. Let me have a talk to him for you; see what I can do.'

Mandy noticed that John, who was quite small himself, easily reached Sara's shoulder. She was a shy, bright, bird-like woman.

'If you leave it a day or two, perhaps I can talk him round,' she suggested.

John hung his head. He was silent.

Oh no! Mandy thought. She half expected to see John rush off again.

But he kept his head low and stood there thinking. 'It wouldn't do any good,' he said at last.

'How do you know? You could let me have a go at least.' Sara spoke gently, pushing her loose hair back behind her ears.

'What for?' he demanded. He looked her straight in the eye. 'Do you like rabbits, or something?'

Sara's face broke into a smile. 'As a matter of fact, yes! I had some myself when I was a kid!'

'Hmm,' John scuffed at the table leg. He hung his head again, then sighed. 'No thanks, don't bother.'

Mandy frowned. She wanted to shake some common sense into him, but she knew how upset he must be.

'Why not? Since I'm going to be living here after the wedding, I could easily take care of a couple of little rabbits when you're away. No problem!'

'They won't always be little!' John broke in scornfully. 'They'll grow. And anyway, I said no thanks!'

'OK.' Sara backed off, ready to retreat into the bar.

'Anyway, you'd never be able to persuade him. You don't know my dad like I do. Once he's made up his mind, he never changes it!' He gave her a haughty look, back to his old buttoned-up self. 'Come on, James, you haven't seen the latest photographs. Have you got five minutes to come up and have a look?' He went off, quietly accepting his father's decision.

Mandy shot a wide-eyed look in Sara's direction.

'Time for a juice?' Sara asked.

Mandy nodded. John was hard to work out. What had happened to his bubbly excitement over Button and Barney? He seemed just to have swallowed it as he led James up the narrow stairs.

'I'm not getting any better at it, am I?' Sara sighed and stared out through the back door. Tiny pink and white blossom flowers framed their view of the old-fashioned walled garden. 'Julian and I get married in June, during John's half-term holiday, but I'm beginning to think he'll even refuse to show up for the wedding!'

'I just think it takes a long time to get to know him,' Mandy admitted.

'If ever!' Sara sighed again and shrugged.

'What happened to his real mum?' Mandy asked. As far back as she could remember, there had always been just John and his dad at the Fox and Goose.

'It was very sad. She was badly injured in a motorway crash. She was unconscious in hospital for five months, then she died.'

Mandy greeted the news in silence.

Sara continued in a slow, quiet voice. 'From what your mum has told me about it, Julian and John got quite a lot of money from the insurance firm after the crash. It helps to pay John's school fees and so on. But of course it never made up for losing his mum.'

Mandy nodded. She felt tears come to her eyes, hot and shining. '*My* real mum and dad were killed in a car crash,' she said at last. 'I'm adopted. I was only a baby when it happened, so I don't remember.'

'So was John. In fact the crash happened before he was born. He was lucky to survive.'

Mandy nodded. Now she understood much more about John's moods; his long silences, his serious gaze. 'Does he like his school?' she asked, trying to find something good to say about the whole sad situation.

But Sara shook her head. 'Not much. It's because Julian has to work all hours in the pub;

he feels John gets a better deal away at Grange. And between you and me, I think poor John feels a bit guilty about not liking school as much as he should. After all, it was his mother's death that paid for it.'

Mandy nodded and sighed. 'Yes, poor John.'

She felt Sara give her a quick hug and saw her brush a forefinger across her own lashes.

'Never mind, perhaps things will work out in the end,' Sara said quietly as James and John came back downstairs.

John gave her a cool stare and walked on out of the house. 'I'm on my way up to High Cross. Does anyone feel like coming along?' he said to James and Mandy in his distant, couldn't-care-less way.

Next day, it was James's idea to head back to the Fox and Goose after they'd helped Mr Hope on his afternoon round. 'Let's see how John's getting on,' he suggested.

Mandy readily agreed.

They found Mr Hardy busy shifting crates and stacking them by the side door, ready for collection. John was up at High Cross again, he told them. 'I don't know what's got into him lately.' He shook his head, and stared into the distance.

Mandy glanced at James. 'Did he go back to the pet shop to tell them he can't have Button and Barney after all?' she asked.

Mr Hardy shook his head. 'I've been thinking about that, though. Maybe I was a bit harsh,' he confessed.

'Here, here!' Sara popped her head round the door, a smile on her face. She grinned at Mandy and James. 'Hello, you two! That's just what I was thinking!' she told her fiancé. She put a cardboard box full of crisps on a nearby table and came out to join them. 'You could still change your mind, Julian. Give John a chance

to look after those rabbits. It'll do him good.'

'Hmm.' Mr Hardy frowned.

Mandy showed James her fingers crossed behind her back. John's dad seemed to be weakening.

Sara went confidently on. 'He's proved it's not just a whim,' she reminded Julian Hardy. 'Rabbits mean an awful lot to John. He really cares. OK, so he shouldn't have gone ahead and paid for Button and Barney without asking you first. I agree about that. But he was obviously carried away. Poor kid. I can't get his face out of my mind when you told him he couldn't bring them home!' She paused.

Me neither! Mandy thought. There was the hurt look, then the blank expression came down like a shutter. 'Poor John,' she said under her breath.

'OK, OK!' Mr Hardy put up his hands to defend himself. He sighed. 'I was only thinking how hard things had been up till now. I mean, having pets really was out of the question before I met you, Sara. I didn't have time for anything except work!'

Sara went up and put an arm round his waist.

'But now?' James prompted. He stood alongside Mandy with his own fingers crossed.

Mr Hardy's face broke into a smile. 'Now it's

different! Now we can all muck in together. And rabbits are pretty straightforward to look after, aren't they?' He turned to Mandy.

'Nothing to it!' she vowed. 'You just have to keep them clean, warm and well fed!'

'OK, that does it!' He gave Sara a hug. 'I've changed my mind. Button and Barney can come!'

James leapt in the air like a footballer who'd scored a winning goal. Mandy shot straight off across the carpark.

'Hang on, where are you going?' James yelled.

'To tell John, of course! I can, can't I?' She checked with his dad.

Everyone grinned. 'Yes, go on! Run up to High Cross and tell him the good news!' Mr Hardy agreed. 'And tell him to get himself back down here. It looks like it's going to rain before too long!'

They ran straight through the village, and up the hill to the remote farm. Then they headed quickly for the far pasture, to John's favourite look-out spot.

There, by the wide bole of an old ash tree, they found his purple and green rucksack propped on top of his green jacket. But there was no sign of John himself.

'He must have gone across to the nursery

warren,' Mandy said. She peeked inside the bag, surprised to see that he'd left his expensive camera unguarded. He was getting careless. She knew that he was determined to study and record each stage of the baby rabbits' progress, but he ought to have taken more care about his belongings.

Mandy and James strode along the wall side, careful to steer clear of the area where the yearlings had set up a new warren. Mandy was bursting to give John the good news about Button and Barney. 'Where's he got to?' she whispered, as they made their way across to the nursery.

They wove their way through five or six low hawthorn trees at the far end of Lydia's pasture. Beyond that, there was a low, rocky ridge running up to the moor top at right angles to it. It made a white ledge that dipped down into rough, unfarmed land. Few people strayed beyond this point, just the odd walker and one or two sheep farmers with their dogs, so the rabbits used it as a safe, quiet place to rear their young. Mandy stood on the ridge and put her hand to her eyes to scan the horizon. She was downwind of the warren, and knew that she was too far away to disturb the rabbits at their evening feed.

Where are you, John? Mandy was starting to feel impatient with him for not being in any of the usual places. Heavy, cold drops of rain began to fall. They made dark blotches on the white rock. She zipped up her jacket against the wind. In the distance she could see a dozen or so adult does hopping uneasily out of their burrows; ears up, back legs kicking. She knew they didn't like the rain, but she guessed there was something extra in the air which made them nervous. None of the babies had followed their mothers into the open. Mandy and James squatted to watch them.

Soon they spotted a few rabbits busily scratching openings in a patch of loose, bare earth, close to a hawthorn tree. They were making new burrows for their litters. But they too kept stopping, sitting up and glancing round, ready to bolt.

'What is it? What's happening?' James whispered. They listened hard for any unusual sound.

Maybe John was hiding upwind of the rabbits by mistake. 'Perhaps they can smell him,' Mandy suggested.

An explosion ripped through the air. High and sharp, it rattled down the hillside from the ridge above. Mandy felt her stomach lurch as she recognised the sound of farmers' guns. The rabbits scattered in an instant. They were gone. The hillside stood eerily empty.

A figure started up from behind a rock. It was John. He began to run up the hill. More gunshots echoed down the valley side.

'John!' Mandy stood and yelled as loud as she could. She and James set off after him.

Another shot cracked through the dull air above. 'John, wait!' she yelled. The wind caught her voice and whipped it back down the hillside into the valley bottom.

He ran, fast as a hare, over the rough ground. The rain had brought down a mist which clung to the ridge and hid the men with the shotguns. Soon John too was a pale figure vanishing into the mist.

'Come back, you'll get shot!' The stuttering guns rattled on. The men were out to get rabbits, to thin down their numbers. Farmers hated rabbits on their land; they ate crops and ruined the soil.

Mandy and James ran and stumbled up the hill. Their breath became short, their legs weakened. They just managed to keep John in view as he leapt over rocks, across rough grass; head back, feet pounding over the distance between him and the sound of guns. He was yelling at them to stop.

Another gust of wind swirled the mist clear of the ground. A dog barked and growled. Mandy saw the black outlines of three men with shotguns to their shoulders, standing on the ridge. Their barrels were tilted down towards the nursery warren. John hurtled straight at them.

Mandy jumped down a drop of about a metre, from a boulder on to a soft bed of couch grass. She stumbled forward, then pushed herself on after John. Nothing would stop him. He seemed to have lost his senses, still running, and only seconds away from the men on the ridge.

'Hold it, there's a kid down there!' the nearest man warned. They let their guns drop to waist height. But they stood, feet planted wide apart, glaring at John. One kept a squat white bulldog close to heel. It growled and bared its teeth as John kept on coming.

'You want to get yourself killed?' the first man yelled in a rough voice. 'Because you're going the right way about it down there!'

John ran at him. 'Don't shoot the rabbits!' He was beside himself with fright.

The man braced himself. He slung his gun over

his shoulder. 'Now, steady on!' he shouted. 'Just hold it where you are. We've got a job to do here, and we aim to do it. So just stand out of our way, sonny, and let us get on with it!'

Six

Mandy didn't stop to think. Her long legs carried her swiftly over the last stretch of rough ground. John had got himself into deep trouble with the men with the guns. She went straight at him from behind, flung herself forward and threw her arms round his waist. She tackled him to the ground.

The first man strode down the hill towards them. The bulldog growled and snapped. James caught up with Mandy and began to pull her and John to their feet. Mandy could feel her heart thumping, her knees hurting from the heavy fall. Still she clung on to John, in case he struggled up and kept on charging. But he stood there gasping, his head turned away.

'All right, all right, just calm down!' The man came down and seized John roughly by the elbow. 'Will someone tell me what the heck's going on round here?' He glared at Mandy and James.

Mandy recognised the thin, sharp features of Dennis Saville, the farm manager at Upper Welford Hall. He was the right-hand man of the owner, Sam Western. She knew him as a hard-hearted, no-nonsense sort who simply carried out his boss's orders. No doubt Mr Western had sent Dennis and a couple of lads up on to the ridge with orders to thin down the local rabbit population.

'It's OK, let me talk to John,' she said. She stooped to brush herself down. She and John were covered in dirt. His face was marked and scratched, and he still struggled as Dennis tried to restrain him.

Another figure, one of the two stocky lads in jeans and heavy boots, came lumbering down the hill. He held his gun under his arm and kicked loose stones as he pulled himself up short alongside Mandy's little group. 'What's up?' he demanded. 'Has the kid gone nuts or something?'

'No!' James was stung into a reply. 'Just leave

him alone, will you? He was only doing what he could to save the rabbits!'

'What?' the lad jeered, as if unable to believe his ears. 'Save rabbits? You must be joking!'

'It's their nursery warren down there, full of babies!' Mandy reminded him.

'So?' The lad stood with one hand in the pocket of his denim jacket, letting the shiny steel barrel of his shotgun drop forward. The polished wooden butt rested under his arm.

'They're just a few weeks old. They're still helpless!'

'So?' He stood and sneered. 'All the better for us!'

John shoved his shoulder against Dennis Saville's chest to try and push him off. His face was drained and white, with a bright red graze on one cheek where he'd fallen against a rough stone.

'Steady on!' Dennis insisted. He was wiry and strong, and kept a firm hold of John's arm. John beat at his tight grasp with his spare hand. 'Now if you don't calm down, I'll set the dog on you!' the manager threatened. Above them, the second lad held the bulldog by its steel-studded collar. It crouched low, ready to leap forward.

'John!' Mandy pleaded. She caught hold of his sleeve. 'Wait a minute, let's just try to explain!' She waited for him to stop pushing, and watched, as slowly the older man released him.

John's breath came out in harsh gasps. His chest and shoulders heaved, but he looked stunned now, rather than wild with fear. His hands shook as he tried to brush mud from his sweater.

'Mr Saville, John's doing a study on the rabbits for a school project. He's been hard at work up here for more than a week now.' She tried to sound calm and reasonable.

The man allowed his frown to relax a fraction. 'Has he now? Yes, that'd be right. I've seen him coming by the big house with his camera often enough. Does Miss Fawcett know you're here? You'd need her permission to cross that last field.'

'Yes, she knows.' Mandy could see that John was still too shocked to answer.

The lad laughed out loud. 'Not much use expecting her to take a gun to a few rabbits,' he scoffed. '*She* probably feeds 'em dandelions and invites 'em in the house. She's as daft as a brush, just like him!' He pointed with the gun at John. 'They're both off their heads, if you ask me!'

'Dean, that'll do!' Dennis Saville warned. 'What

Lydia Fawcett gets up to on her own land is her business, and we can't do a thing about it if she chooses not to shoot rabbits. But this is common land, and up here we've every right to try and cut down on this year's young 'uns.'

'But why?' Mandy pleaded. 'What harm are they doing to you if they dig their warren way up here?'

Dennis Saville gave an exasperated sigh. 'They don't stay put here on this stretch, do they now? Soon as they've found their feet these young ones come scampering down to the Hall, looking for whatever they can find. Nice juicy fruit from the currant bushes, anything they can sink their teeth into, little devils. And they dig up the lawn and make a right mess of things. Can you blame Mr Western for wanting to get rid of them?'

Mandy wasn't convinced. She thought a rabbit had as much right to be where he or she wanted as any local landowner. But she bit her tongue. 'Can't you put wire netting round the fruit bushes?' she asked, looking for a logical way out.

Dean snorted and stamped off back up the hill. 'Why are we wasting time with these loonies?' he asked in a loud voice. He released the barrel on his gun, ready to load more shot.

John seemed to come back to life at the sound

of the click of metal. He turned on Dennis Saville. 'You're not going to let them start up again, are you?'

The farm manager shrugged. 'Listen, why don't you three just move off back to High Cross for half an hour? There'll be plenty of rabbits left for you to carry on studying, even after we've finished here.'

Mandy felt her blood run cold. She turned to James. 'Tell them that's not the point!' The mist was lifting and the clouds rolling away. Soon the rabbits would get back their nerve and emerge from the nursery warren.

'It's no use, they won't listen!' James turned and walked three or four paces downhill. 'But it's just like you said,' he told the farm manager. 'This is common ground. We've got as much right to be here as you lot. And we're not shifting! This is where we're staying, right here!' He stood and glared back up the hill. Behind and below him, the land kept its eerie silence.

'Good idea!' Mandy followed his lead. 'Come on, John! If they won't listen to reason, we'll have to find another way of stopping them!' She joined James, leaping on to a low boulder, and looking determined to see off the three men with their guns.

Saville stared down at them and shook his head. He put his hands in his pockets and strode back up to the ridge. 'Down! Stay down!' he ordered the dog. For a few moments he stood and talked with the two lads.

'I only hope this works!' Mandy whispered to John and James.

'Well, *I'm* not moving,' John replied between clenched teeth. He stood alongside James and Mandy. 'James is right; we're staying right where we are!'

'Forever?' Mandy bit her bottom lip. What had

they got themselves into now? The men were still discussing their next tactic.

'For as long as *they* stay!' John promised. 'And I'll be here for as long as there's any chance of them coming back!'

'Could be a long wait.' Mandy glanced at him. The wind had brought colour back to his cheeks. His head was up, his face looked brave and clear. 'Anyway, good for you. After tonight we can get Lydia to use her new phone to send down warnings to Animal Ark or to the Fox and Goose, whenever she sees them crossing the back of her place with their guns. It'll mostly be in the evenings. And we'll drop what we're doing and be up here like a shot – oops!' She laughed at her choice of words.

'Great!' The wind blew John's hair straight back. 'As long as we're around they won't be able to shoot any more rabbits!'

'Maybe!' James added, in his sensible, clear way.

They waited, confidence rising, and they watched as Dennis Saville shrugged and muttered one last instruction to the lads. Then he led them and the dog off over the ridge out of sight.

Mandy, James and John cheered. 'Brilliant!' John cried. 'That's the first battle won, at any rate!'

With huge sighs of relief, they ran back to the ash trees and John's usual lookout spot. They crouched down. Soon peace and quiet returned to the high fields. No more gunshots. No more man-smell to scare the rabbits. Now the pasture and the hills beyond were alive with mother and baby rabbits, lolloping, crouching, scuffling, nibbling, nipping, and combing their ears in the calm evening air.

'One more thing!' Mandy said, when she could catch her breath at last. James studied the rabbits with a small, secret grin on his face as he listened to her. 'Ask us why we came up here when we did! Go on, ask us!' She couldn't hide her own excitement at the news she was about to give.

John dragged his own glance away from the rabbits. 'Go on, then. Why?'

'Your dad sent us.'

'Oh!' he grunted.

'To tell you—'

'To get back home for supper?' he growled.

'No! To tell you you can keep Button and Barney after all!'

'Where? At home?' John's mouth hung open. He grabbed hold of Mandy's arm.

'Yes, at home! He changed his mind!'

John whooped and fell flat on his back. 'Tell me I'm not dreaming!' he gasped.

'You're not dreaming. You can keep the rabbits,' James repeated. 'Come on, let's go!'

They gathered John's things, dragged him up off the ground, and headed for home.

But Lydia cut them off as they made their way down past High Cross. 'You three haven't been getting yourselves shot at, have you?' she called. 'I heard all the noise up there!' She came up to them with a worried frown.

'No!' Mandy laughed. 'Not quite.' She told Lydia what had happened.

'Hmm.' Lydia was still frowning. 'I'm on your side,' she told them. 'Call me soft-hearted, but I hate the idea of taking a gun to the poor creatures as much as you three do. On the other hand, I don't want you to risk getting yourselves shot!'

'We won't!' James promised. 'But if you do see Dennis Saville up there again, can you ring and tell us? We've got a plan to stop them shooting in the nursery warren.'

Lydia nodded. She took John inside to bathe his grazed face in warm water and disinfectant.

'We just need to be there. That would be enough,' Mandy explained. 'They'd never carry on shooting while we're there.'

'Let me think about it,' Lydia said. 'Perhaps I can come up with a better plan.'

'What?' John winced as she dabbed his graze with cotton-wool.

'Maybe I can get them to give into the temptation of freshly-baked scones whenever they're passing this way. That would soon put paid to their rabbiting; hot tea and fresh scones!' Lydia's eyes twinkled.

'I'm not sure.' John stood up and looked at Mandy and James.

'Well, leave it with me. Perhaps I can think of something else as well.' Lydia drained off the bowl of water at the sink.

Mandy nodded. She could trust her old friend to help them out. 'Come on,' she said, anxious to get John back home.

They said goodbye to Lydia and ran on, down past Upper Welford Hall, then past Beacon House. Mandy waved to Imogen Parker Smythe. The little girl swung moodily to and fro on the swing her father had slung from a branch of one of their huge beech trees. The plump, pig-tailed seven-year-old was slow to wave back. She had her heated swimming-pool and her enormous garden, but she didn't seem to have any friends who would come and play. Mandy usually saw her all alone, scowling, or running inside to her mum, whenever she passed.

Mandy, James and John gathered speed down the steep hill, and ran down past the golf-club, past the tennis-courts, and over the old bridge to the crossroads and the Fox and Goose.

Julian Hardy looked relaxed and comfortable in a blue open-necked shirt as he lounged in front of the television. In the bar, his staff were getting ready for the evening trade. Sara sat at a table by the window. She was writing out wedding invitations on squares of cream-coloured card edged with silver. She looked up and smiled at the three of them, then laid down her pen.

'Hello, son!' Mr Hardy made room for John on the sofa. He put an arm along the back of it, close to his shoulder. 'Hey, have you been in the wars?' he asked. He'd noticed the raw graze on John's cheek.

'I slipped on a rock, that's all,' John said. 'Something had scared the rabbits, and I was just trying to sort it out when I slipped and lost my footing.' He stared meaningfully at Mandy and James, as if to warn them not to go into detail.

'Well, never mind, no real harm done.' Mr Hardy grinned across at Sara. 'When shall we go and collect Barney and Button, then?'

'First thing tomorrow?' she suggested. Mandy could see that Sara was going to enjoy this almost as much as anyone else in the room.

John's grin stretched from ear to ear. 'Fantastic! Thanks, Dad!'

'Thank Mandy and James, and Sara here. She threatened to divorce me if I said no to the rabbits!'

'And we're not even married yet!' she joked.

John turned towards her. 'Thanks, Sara.' He looked round the room at them all. 'Oh, great! Oh, fantastic! Oh, brilliant! . . . Wow!' he said.

Seven

'Nice to see that you two have made friends again,' Jean commented. She peered over her glasses from behind the reception desk at Animal Ark.

James Hunter had arrived early for the trip into Walton. Sara had promised to wait at the Fox and Goose while Mandy and James travelled over to the pet shop with John and his father. She knew they could help choose the right food and so on, so they'd arranged to meet up at the pub at nine o'clock.

Now James coloured up under Jean's gaze.

'We never fell out in the first place!' Mandy objected. 'James has always been my best friend!'

'I've just remembered something! I've got to padlock my bike!' James darted outside.

Mandy flicked her hair back from her forehead. 'See what you've done? You've embarrassed him!'

Jean smiled. 'He's such a nice boy, James Hunter. I was quite lost without him last week, when he went away and you seemed to have taken up with the Hardy boy. I missed his smiling face!' She smiled. Her own grandchildren lived too far away for her to see them often.

'John Hardy is nice too,' Mandy protested. 'Once you get to know him.' She remembered to write a name and phone number into the appointment book from a phone call she'd taken just before James arrived. 'You know, he was great yesterday. He stopped Mr Western's men from shooting all the rabbits up at High Cross!' She delivered the tale of John's heroic dash up the hill. ' . . . And then he came face to face with the barrel of a gun and he never even flinched! Imagine! Only inches away from his nose. It was just like on TV!'

Jean tutted. 'You're exaggerating again, dear.'

'No, I'm not. Oh, well, maybe just a teeny bit! But most of it's true! And now he's going to get the reward he deserves. His dad says he can have the two baby rabbits from the pet shop in town. Isn't that great?'

Jean's eyebrows shot up. 'I thought Julian Hardy had enough on his plate, poor man, coping with everything single-handed.' Jean went to straighten the chairs back against the wall, ready for surgery to begin.

'Well, he won't be single-handed after he marries Sara, will he? And *she* likes pets. And anyway, he did say yes. We were there at the time!' Mandy checked her watch and ran a brush through her hair, getting ready to go.

'Hmm, well, he must be going soft in his old age, then.' Jean chatted on regardless. 'Funny that; rabbits seem to be popular at the moment. I had a phone call only yesterday from someone who wanted to know about inoculations for them, and so on. The little girl was so excited she could hardly get the word out. I told her to bring her rabbits along to the surgery this Saturday.'

'Well, I'm not surprised they're so popular. They're gorgeous creatures.' Mandy thought of the fluffy brown babies in Pets' Parlour, and of her own three rabbits happily munching oats out in the back garden. She glanced out of the window on to the drive. 'Here's Simon now!' She went

out to join James, and they crossed paths with
Animal Ark's young nurse who, as ever, looked
bright and cheerful as he turned up for work.

'Don't do anything I wouldn't do!' he called
after them.

'As if!' Mandy replied. They were in high spirits
themselves as they headed for the Fox and Goose.

They rode over to Walton in Mr Hardy's smart
green car. John sat in the front, silent with
excitement, almost gripping the sides of his seat
in his eagerness to be there. No one said much
during the fifteen minute journey; they just looked
out across the moor, spotting curlews overhead,
plus the odd seagull, and high above, a sparrow-
hawk gliding on the air currents.

Mr Hardy parked in the town's central carpark.
Together they crossed the main street. Mandy
waved at Mr Cecil, hard at work inside his
chocolate shop. He was filling the windows with
home-made chocolate assortment boxes. Down
the road they could spot the red lettering over
the window of Pets' Parlour, and the much
dimmer, more cluttered interior.

'Come on!' John insisted, breaking into a run
for the last few metres.

They looked into the window at the muddle of dog leads, baskets, mice cages and budgerigar mirrors. There was a gap where Button and Barney should have been. John shot an anxious look at his father.

'They must still be inside,' Mr Hardy remarked. 'Having breakfast. Come on, let's go in and see.' He opened the door to the stuffy smell of birdseed and fish food. Across the dark room, the blue, red and silver fishes darted across their bubbling tank. James was the last one in. He closed the door to the loud tinkle of the shop bell.

'Yes, please? Can I help you?' Geoff, the friendly young shopkeeper, came out from the back room, his red shirt covered in stray wisps of straw, his sleeves rolled back. 'I hope I didn't keep you waiting.'

Julian Hardy nudged John forward to the counter. Mandy and James stayed quietly in the background. Their eyes swept the shelves for any sign of the rabbit hutch. A nervous feeling had begun to clutch hold of Mandy's stomach.

'I've come about the rabbits,' John began. He put both hands on the counter to steady his nerves.

Geoff studied him more closely. 'I'm sorry,

which rabbits?' He looked puzzled.

John carried on. 'I know it must have seemed a bit strange, me not coming straight back for them yesterday, but can I collect them now, please? I'd like to take them home.'

Mr Hardy stepped forward to help out. 'Actually, to be fair, it was me who caused the delay, not John. I thought we wouldn't be able to cope with Button and Barney. But then I thought better of it. He can have them after all, and we promise five-star accommodation at the Fox and Goose!' He jollied the mood, which seemed to have gone awkward and flat.

Behind the counter, Geoff began to frown. 'Button and Barney? The little brown rabbits?' He coughed and cleared the back of his throat, then shook his head.

Mandy's chest thudded; one dreadful, heart stopping moment.

Geoff went on. 'Look, I'm sorry, but you're too late. I'm afraid I've already sold those two, just yesterday afternoon. Don't worry, it was to a very good owner.' He shrugged and looked uncomfortable. 'You're out of luck there, I'm afraid.'

The life drained from John's face. His eyes

stared slowly round the shelves, as if this was some terrible joke and Button and Barney could be found lurking in a dark corner. 'But I already paid for them!' he stammered. 'They were *my* rabbits! You can't have sold them to someone else!'

Mandy saw from the stricken look on her friend's face that his world had collapsed. He stared as Geoff explained what must have happened. 'It wasn't me you bought them from, was it?'

Slowly John shook his head. 'No, it was someone else. A lady.'

Geoff nodded. 'That was Mrs Kearney. She was looking after things in the shop that day. She obviously forgot to tell me that she'd sold the rabbits to you!' He sighed and then shrugged at Julian Hardy. 'I'm very sorry. He's obviously upset, and I don't blame him. It's a bad mistake on our part. But I'll tell you what!' He turned to John. 'I'll put your name to the top of the list, and I'll tell you when the next two rabbits come up for sale. I'm expecting to take in another litter in a couple of weeks,' he said. 'You could come back then. In the meantime, I'll refund your money.'

'I'll be away at school,' John said in a hollow voice.

'But I can bring Mandy and James back here,' his father offered. 'They can help me choose some more rabbits.' He stood, hands in pockets. 'Look, John, it's not a disaster. We can still get you some pets.'

He shook his head. 'No thanks.'

'Why not?'

'Because it's Button and Barney I want. I bought them myself, and I don't feel the same about having any others. Thanks.' He turned stiffly away.

Julian Hardy shrugged at the shopkeeper. 'It looks as though we'll have to leave it for now,' he said.

Geoff nodded. 'Sorry about the mix-up.' He spread his palms and returned the shrug. 'I do feel really bad about it.'

'Never mind, it can't be helped. It doesn't matter.' He smiled and herded James, Mandy and John out of the shop.

Mandy heard the doorbell ring behind them. *Yes, it does matter!* she thought. *It means the whole world to John!*

She glanced at James, uncertain what to do next. Button and Barney had been whisked away from under their noses. She felt empty and sad, and yet she could only guess how disappointed John himself must feel. They trailed back to the carpark in complete silence.

'Sorry,' Mr Hardy sighed, as they sank into their car seats. 'I can see that this is all my fault. I shouldn't have held things up. I really am sorry, John!'

John pulled his seat-belt across his chest. 'Oh no, not at all,' he said. 'It's nobody's fault. It's just one of those things.'

How can he say that? Mandy wondered. She knew John must be feeling dreadful!

When they got back to the Fox and Goose, John got out of the car and went straight to his room. Mandy looked at Mr Hardy, who nodded that she should follow him up. She took the stairs two at a time.

Mandy opened John's bedroom door. He sat cross-legged on the floor. The walls were covered in diagrams and sketches. Rabbits stared down at him from the bathroom door, from his wonderful photographs still scattered all over the carpet. He was surrounded by them. But he hadn't got what he really wanted. All he wanted was Button and Barney to clean and feed and care for. Two live creatures to help him get over the changes that had come charging into his life.

'I thought you might like some company,' said Mandy.

'Thanks, Mandy, but I'd rather be on my own,' John replied in a quiet voice.

'I understand,' Mandy said. 'Call me tomorrow, and we can go up to High Cross together.' John nodded a reply, but Mandy wondered if he really would call. She quietly closed his bedroom door.

Feeling rather helpless, Mandy went downstairs.

After the disaster at the pet shop, Mandy and James didn't hear a word from John. Sara popped into Animal Ark for coffee one morning and told Mandy's mum that he was drifting round the house like a ghost. 'Like he's not really there,' she said. 'And he's out all the time; every chance he gets, he's up roaming round on that farm. His dad's nearly out of his mind with worry. We really don't know what to do.'

Emily Hope gave Sara a sympathetic smile. 'Give him time,' she advised. 'There are so many new things for him to get used to all at once.'

Mrs Hope saw her old school-friend to the door, and shook her head sadly. As she went to begin surgery, Mandy realised that even her mum had no decent solutions.

She heard too from Lydia that John Hardy now spent all his time among the High Cross warrens. Lydia rang up one teatime, worried that she hadn't seen Mandy up there with him during the last few days. 'I thought you might be ill,' she said. 'I got so used to you coming along too that I began to wonder what had happened. Have you two fallen out?'

'No. But John said he wanted to be by himself. He said he can concentrate on his work better that way.' Mandy fiddled with the half eaten cheese-on-toast on her plate. She'd lost her appetite and spent her own time worrying what was happening to John. Lydia's phone call did nothing to put her mind at rest.

'Hmm. It's not good for a boy of his age to be alone so much.' Lydia let a big pause develop before she went on. 'Mandy, I don't suppose you could—'

She jumped in without allowing Lydia to finish. 'Come up to High Cross? Yes, of course I can. James is here too. We'll both be right up!' She jumped to her feet and looked in James's direction.

'Oh, good. I'm sure it'll help to cheer him up. He looks so . . . lonely, you know. It's very cut off up here. I'm sure he'd prefer to have some company.'

'OK?' Mandy signalled to James. He nodded. 'OK, Lydia, we're on our way.' She put down the phone. Whether or not John would prefer to have company, Mandy leapt at Lydia's suggestion.

She and James hopped on to their bikes and pedalled up the hill. It was evening; John was certain to be hanging round the warrens at this time of day. The rabbits would be feeding and basking in the low sun. That, anyway, would be a sight worth seeing.

Sure enough, John's rucksack sat abandoned at the foot of the ash tree. Down past the farm, they could see Lydia leading the goats in for milking. Then, higher up, beyond the far pasture, they spotted John. He sat still as a statue on a low rock, huddled over a sketchbook. All round him rabbits grazed, nipping and nibbling at the grass. The hillside would spring to life whenever they moved; hopping, kicking and darting to the next juicy leaf. John was there right in their midst, but they ignored him.

'He looks like part of the scenery,' James

whispered. 'I bet he wishes he could stay here forever.'

'Poor John,' Mandy sighed. 'Let's wait here until he moves. We don't want to scare them all away.' They stood by a wall, watching and waiting.

When the rabbits sat bolt upright, twitching their ears to listen out for danger, Mandy and James saw John glance behind. There must have been a tiny sound, up over the horizon. The rabbits stared and twitched. Another sound. They fled. Dozens of white tails bobbed and were gone. John stood up and turned to face the high ridge.

Two figures appeared. They carried shotguns and swaggered down the hill.

'Dean and his friend!' Mandy gasped. She ran forward across the empty pasture. 'Not again!' But this time there was no farm manager to keep the lads in check.

'I think that's Steve Burnley with him,' James told her.

The two youths were bearing down on John, who just stood waiting, camera round his neck, sketchbook at his side.

'He got expelled for bullying in his last year. I know his younger brother, Frankie.' James sounded worried. 'Have you seen their guns?'

'Yes, and I've got this feeling that John's likely to do something rash again, the strange mood he's been in lately!' Mandy began to shout and wave her arms, trying to distract Dean and Steve's attention.

But John turned on them as they clambered over the last low wall on to the common ground. 'Go away!' he yelled. 'I can deal with this!'

On a level with John, Dean came to a halt. 'Not you again!' he said scornfully. 'I've had just about enough of you!'

'Tough!' John retorted. 'Because I'm not moving!'

Dean laughed. 'Big man!'

John stood his ground.

Dean's friend, Steve, curled his lip and took up position on the far side of John.

'Wait!' James warned Mandy. 'Better see what happens next!' He pulled her to a halt.

'I said I'm not moving!' John insisted. His chin was up, he stared back at them.

'Do you think we can't make you!' Dean taunted. He tapped the barrel of his gun, then grinned.

James and Mandy gasped.

'Look, sonny, just stand out of the way, why don't you?' Steve advised. 'We've got a job to do here; Mr Western's orders. And we always do what we're told, don't we, Dean?' Swiftly he swung his gun round in the direction of some distant hawthorns. He took a shot at them. The sound cracked and echoed across the valley.

Mandy jumped, but John didn't move a muscle. She half turned away, afraid to look.

'Go on, shoot! But I'm still not moving!' he yelled. 'I'm staying right where I am!'

'Now, no one's shooting anything round here!' A calm voice started up close by, just behind James. Lydia had marched up from the bottom pasture, leading Houdini on a short rope. The goat's head was down, horns at the ready. He'd picked up Lydia's serious tone. 'I suggest you two just put away those guns, and listen to me for a minute.'

John waved them back. 'I'm not moving from this spot!'

'Who said anything about moving?' Lydia said mildly. But she stood firm, Houdini at her side. Dean glanced at the goat and frowned at Steve. Together they backed off a step or two. 'I expect you'd like a word of explanation,' Lydia continued. 'I can see that this must all be rather puzzling. Now, I want you two to go back to Mr Western and tell him this piece of news.'

Steve's lip curled again. 'What's she on about?'

Dean shrugged, but he didn't dare speak. Houdini stared him in the eye.

Lydia drew a brownish paper from her work jacket pocket and began to open it out.

'What I have here is a map of High Cross land,' she explained. 'Dating from the time when my grandfather farmed here. Now, it's an old map but it's a good one.' She beckoned Dean and Steve across. Reluctantly they went and bowed their stubbly heads over Lydia's paper.

'I had some idea that Mr Western and Dennis

Saville might be mistaken,' Lydia went on. 'So I went to my desk the other day and unearthed this map, just in case. See – I was right!' She pointed a finger at a faint dotted line. 'The High Cross boundary cuts across the ridge and down by those hawthorns over there. That means the area where we're standing isn't common land after all!'

Mandy took a deep breath of surprise and relief.

Lydia looked from Steve to Dean. 'You can see for yourselves, it's High Cross land.'

Dean ducked his head and grunted. 'But Mr Western says we have to keep back the rabbits,' he complained.

'That may well be,' Lydia agreed. She folded the map and put it back in her pocket. 'And you have to follow orders whenever you can; I can see that. But not on *my* land, you don't!' She looked calmly at them. 'So you'd best go back and tell Mr Western that from me. Tell him it may not be worth anything as farming land, but I fancy it does rather well as an old-fashioned nature reserve. There's every variety of clover, wild cowslip, and that pretty pale lilac flower which we called milkmaids when I was young. Besides, there's the rabbit nursery.' She smiled at John, then gazed gently round. 'And

this is the way I like it, just as it was in Grandfather's time!'

Dean and Steve knew when they were beaten.
If nothing else, they didn't like the look of
Houdini's sharp horns. 'OK, OK,' Dean said, as
the goat stamped and strained at his rope, 'we're
on our way. We'll tell him, then he can't blame
us.' He muttered to Steve as they backed off; 'It's
not my fault if he lives next door to a rabbit lover,
is it? It's nothing to do with me.'

Lydia kept on smiling and nodding at John,
Mandy and James as the two lads made their way
back up the hill, guns drooping, shoulders
hunched. 'Well done, Houdini!' she said proudly.

He tossed his head and stamped.

'Is all that true?' Mandy demanded. She pointed
to the map bulging in Lydia's pocket. 'How come
you made this discovery all of a sudden?'

Lydia's eyes crinkled shrewdly. 'According to
this map, it's true; we're standing on High Cross
land.'

'But?' Mandy knew Lydia well enough to know
there was more to it.

'But Grandfather was an argumentative sort.
He had the map drawn up in a dispute against
Mr Western's own grandfather. This was over sixty

years ago. And as far as I know, the two old gentlemen never settled their quarrel, and the dispute is still in the hands of some dusty lawyer's clerk.' She laughed mischievously.

'In other words?' James said.

'In other words, I don't know whose land it is!' Lydia smiled broadly. 'But those two weren't to know that, were they? And it'll take Sam Western many months to go back to the lawyers and work it all out to his satisfaction. If he can be bothered to go to all that expense over a piece of rough old land like this!'

'Lydia!' James and Mandy chorused together. They hopped around at the success of her little scheme.

Quietly, John bent to pick up his pencil. 'Thank you very much, Miss Fawcett,' he said. he stood awkwardly. 'Thanks, James. Thanks, Mandy.'

His words set a seal on the incident, and now it was plain that he wanted to be by himself again. He sat back on the rock and bent his head over his work.

Lydia nodded for James and Mandy to come away. 'Give him time,' she advised. 'I think that's what he needs.'

That's what everyone says, Mandy thought. *But it doesn't seem to work!*

She and James followed Lydia and Houdini through the long grass. 'He doesn't have any more time,' Mandy told her. 'He goes back to school on Sunday, and I'm really worried about him.' She turned to James. 'You see what I mean about him? It's like he's locked himself up and thrown away the key. I don't think he can ever bear to speak about losing Button and Barney!'

James nodded. They came to a halt in the farmyard.

'What would it take to put things right?' Lydia asked Mandy. 'You know John better than most, I suspect.'

Mandy sighed. 'Button and Barney,' she replied. 'That's what it would take. But they were sold to someone else by mistake earlier in the week.'

They stood together in the dusk.

'I've got it!' James said suddenly. 'If Button and Barney are the only things that'll help, what we have to do is set out and find them, isn't it?' He looked eagerly at Mandy. 'See? If we found the lucky owners and tracked the rabbits down, at least John would know where they were. We might even be able to get them back for him!'

Mandy saw it in a flash; James was right.
'Sometimes I could hug you, James Hunter!' she
cried, with a mad urge to fling her arms round
him. 'You have the best ideas!'

Lydia laughed as James ducked and darted away.
'Keep her off me!' he yelped.

'Don't worry, you're safe!' Mandy spread her
arms wide and spun round on the spot like
Superwoman. 'Da-da! Let the quest to find Button
and Barney begin!' she announced. 'Pets' Parlour,
here we come!'

Eight

James and Mandy were waiting on the doorstep of Pets' Parlour when Geoff turned up looking rumpled and sleepy. It was half-past eight in the morning.

'Hi, it's us again!' Mandy said. 'I bet you wish you could get rid of us!'

He grinned, opened the door and invited them into the shop. 'So what can I do for you this time?' Geoff hung his keys on a hook behind the counter and flicked the switch on a kettle which sat on a nearby shelf. 'Go ahead, talk to me. But don't expect me to take much in at this time in the morning. Not until I've had a cup of coffee!'

'Don't worry, we'll be quick,' James promised. 'We just need a little bit of information.'

Mandy took a pen and piece of paper out of her jacket pocket. She looked up eagerly, ready to scribble down the name and address of Button and Barney's new owners.

Geoff rubbed the top of his tousled head and yawned. 'OK, try me!' He nodded to a middle-aged woman with curly brown hair who'd just followed them into the shop. 'Morning, Mrs Kearney!' he said.

'Can you tell us who took the baby rabbits that John Hardy had bought?' James blurted out. 'You see, he bought them first, so it's him who should really have them, isn't it? And we thought we might be able to track them down for him.'

Mandy's pen hovered over the paper.

Geoff looked doubtful. 'I don't know about that . . .'

'It's OK, we're not planning to go off and kidnap them. Or bunnynap them!' James promised. 'But we did think we could talk to the other buyers and see if they would let John have the rabbits back.'

'They might agree, once they hear the full story,' Mandy put in.

'Maybe you're right.' Geoff frowned and shook his head. 'And I can see that you two wouldn't go and do anything daft.' He glanced again at Mrs Kearney who was just buttoning up her overall, ready to start her day's work.

'Then what's the problem?' James glanced anxiously at Mandy. Their plan seemed to be coming to a full stop before it had begun.

'The problem is, I can't tell you exactly who went off with Button and Barney. These people came into the shop, chose them and paid cash for them. They didn't even give me their name.'

Mandy's hopes came crashing down. She stuffed the pen and paper back into her pocket, at a loss for words.

James was deep in thought. 'But what did they look like, these people? Do they ever come in here for other things? Won't they be coming back to buy food and bedding for the rabbits? Haven't you seen them round town since? Don't you have a clue who they might be?'

'Whoa, steady on!' Geoff held up his hands in protest. 'One thing at a time!' He poured milk into his coffee and stirred it. 'I can tell you what they looked like, but I don't know if it will help much. They were a fairly ordinary couple, a man and wife. I can't say I noticed that much about them. He was tall and well-dressed. She was neat and slim, and well-groomed. I think she was wearing gold earrings. She had blonde hair. His hair was darker, I think.'

'Didn't they have a child with them?' Mandy forced her brain into action, once she was over the first disappointment.

Geoff shook his head. 'No. They wanted to buy the rabbits as a surprise Easter present for their little girl. It was very hush-hush. Apparently she'd been wanting a pet for ages. They were passing by and thought Button and Barney would be just the thing. Easter bunnies.'

James sighed. 'You were right, it doesn't help much. And you're sure you've never seen them before?'

'I swear. But like you say, they might come back for rabbit food and so on. I could always find out more for you then.'

Mandy shook her head. 'No, today's Saturday. John goes off to school tomorrow. We have to track these people down today, to try and get Button and Barney back before he leaves home. That's the plan at any rate.'

All three looked at one another. Mrs Kearney stood in the background, looking uncomfortable. 'Don't worry, nobody's blaming you!' Geoff called out. 'It's just been a bit of bad luck, that's all.'

A gloomy feeling had settled on Mandy.

'Thanks.' Mandy nodded and smiled briefly. 'Thanks for all your help.'

'No worries. Sorry it didn't work out.'

The bell rang as they left the shop. Mandy turned, one foot on the step. 'Oh, we haven't given up,' she promised. 'Not by a long way! This is just a small setback. We've got all day to sort it out!' She closed the door and stepped down on to the street. She breathed in deeply as she zipped her jacket.

'OK, next idea?' James asked. They passed a newspaper shop, Cecil's Confectionery and a chemist's. People queued outside a bread shop, waiting for it to open.

'We could advertise in all the shops,' Mandy suggested. The cards in the newsagents' window had brought this to mind. 'You know; a message in the Wanted section. "Wanted: two brown rabbits from Pets' Parlour. Would the new owners please contact Animal Ark, Welford

703267." If they ring up, we can tell them the whole story.'

'It's worth a try,' James agreed. So they spent half an hour going up and down the High Street, writing out cards and paying to stick them on clear display in all the newsagents' windows and on the notice-board in the town library. 'It's a weekend, so town should be busy,' James said hopefully. 'Plenty of people will read the notices!'

'The trouble is, we don't have much time.' Mandy stood back from the library notice-board. 'What now?' she said with a sigh.

'I suppose we could go over to York. There are loads more pet shops there. We could try them all to see if they've got any brown baby rabbits that look the same as Button and Barney. Then we could go back and tell John we'd found them after all!'

'You mean, *lie*?' Mandy took a deep breath.

'It's only a white lie. And it's for a good cause.'

'I know. But it's a bit risky, isn't it?'

'Shh!' The assistant behind the polished wooden counter pointed to a notice above their heads. It read, 'Silent Reading Area'.

Mandy and James blushed and slunk out of

the library. They stood on the street, opposite the railway station, wondering whether to risk a trip to York. 'Do you think we'd get away with it?' Mandy asked. 'I mean, John is a real rabbit expert now. He's bound to notice the difference. You know what he's like. He probably knows every whisker and hair on Button and Barney's head.'

James sighed. 'You're right. Anyway, I just realised; I spent all my money on those Wanted cards. I couldn't afford to go to York on the train, even if we decided it was worth a try.'

'Me neither. I've only got enough for the bus back to Welford.' Mandy felt another emergency plan flare and fade. 'If only we weren't so short of time!' Tomorrow John would pack his huge suitcase and drag it across the carpark at the Fox and Goose. He'd be off to school, then home again at half-term for the wedding. But there'd be no pet rabbits sitting cosily in his back garden under the apple tree.

'I suppose we'd better go back home,' James decided. 'We've done all we can here. I can't think of another single thing!'

She was forced to agree. 'John will be up at High Cross already, you realise? He'll stay until dark, all by himself, with his rabbits and his sketch-book and camera.'

'I know.' They both sighed.

'I'd like to go and join him, but I don't think I can face him just yet,' Mandy decided.

'It's his last day.'

'I know. But let's go back to Animal Ark first and have one final think about it. I need to tell Jean about our Wanted notices, just in case someone rings up. After that, what do you say we take sandwiches and biscuits up to High Cross? I bet John hasn't even thought of that. He's bound to be hungry.'

James nodded, and they climbed, heavy-hearted, on to the Welford bus. It wasn't often they had to give in where animals were concerned. They could find good homes for kittens, and put up strong fences for goats. They could rescue orphan hedgehogs. But they couldn't magic the twin rabbits out of thin air, and they couldn't make one sad boy happy.

'Cheer up; the holiday isn't over yet, you know!' Mandy's dad called as he climbed into his Land-rover to set off on his morning round. He gave James and Mandy a cheerful wave.

Mandy could hardly raise a smile.

Mr Hope wound down the window and studied her serious face. 'Tell me about it later. Or talk to Mum after surgery. I'm sure we can sort something out.'

Not this time, Mandy thought. She tried to smile back at him. 'Thanks, Dad.' They went inside, to the busy waiting area of Animal Ark.

Toby, Mrs Ponsonby's mongrel dog, came tottering out of a treatment room. He wore a big white plastic cone around his head and looked very sorry for himself. The cone knocked clumsily against the doorpost and he yelped.

'Oh, poor Toby! Poor doggy!' His fussy, middle-aged owner bent to scoop him off the floor. 'Did he hurt his poor little self? Oh, diddums!' She hugged him, and staggered out across reception.

'What's he done to himself?' Mandy stroked Toby gently on the nose. She could see a small, open sore on the dog's back. Mandy knew he had to wear the plastic cone to stop him from nipping at it and making it even worse.

Mrs Ponsonby raised her arched eyebrows from behind her fancy pink glasses and mouthed a secret word: 'Fleabite!'

'Oh, dear!' Mandy sympathised. She knew how they itched. 'Did he go and scratch it too hard?'

'Shh, dear! Yes, I'm afraid Toby was a naughty little doggy!' He wasn't so little. Mrs Ponsonby's legs had begun to buckle under his weight.

'Here, let me help,' Mandy offered. She took the miserable mongrel and set him down on his own four feet. Then she led him carefully out to Mrs Ponsonby's car. 'Don't worry, that wound will soon clear up. It's nice and clean now. It should be better in a few days, then Toby will be good as new!'

'Thank you, Mandy dear!' Mrs Ponsonby stowed her precious dog into the special compartment at the back of her car. She tugged at the jacket of her powder-blue suit to straighten it, then fixed her straw hat more firmly on her head. 'I must say, you're not looking quite yourself today, dear. You're a bit peaky. Is there something the matter?'

'No, I'm fine, Mrs Ponsonby. Thanks!' Mandy helped her to close the back door on Toby. 'I've got a problem on my mind, that's all.' She waved and went inside once more.

On the doorstep, she paused to see who was

turning into their drive as Mrs Ponsonby drove out. 'Oh no!' she groaned out loud. 'Just what I need!'

'Trouble?' Jean asked. She was wearing a flowery dress in white, blue and green, with big white buttons down the front. She looked summery and breezy, but surrounded as usual by a muddle of opened letters, papers, catalogues and bills.

James came across to the door. 'Uh-oh!' His mouth turned down at the corners. 'What are *they* doing here?'

'Exactly!' Mandy's eyes narrowed. She watched as Mr Parker Smythe stepped out of his posh black car and came towards the surgery.

'Since when did they need a vet?' James wondered. Both Mandy and he were only too well aware that the family owned a tennis-court, a helicopter and a swimming-pool. But as far as they knew, they had no pets.

'Hello,' the tall man said. His thinning hair was smartly combed, and he wore a posh grey suit. He looked strict, but he spoke to them pleasantly as he strolled into reception.

Mandy stared hard at his car. Inside, sitting behind tinted glass windows, she spied the blonde head of Mrs Parker Smythe and the chubbier shape of Imogen's pale face. To Mandy's surprise, the girl was actually looking cheerful. She pressed a button to slide down the window, then leaned out eagerly, watching for her father's return.

In the reception area, Jean was talking to Imogen's dad. 'That's quite right, Mr Parker Smythe. Your appointment with Mrs Hope is for ten o'clock. Just bring them inside and take a seat over there. I'm sure you'll be seen shortly.'

Mandy and James slid inside the reception room as Mr Parker Smythe came out. 'Jean, what are they doing here? What's going on?' Mandy whispered. 'I never knew Imogen had a pet!'

'Ah, you wait and see,' Jean replied, smiling sweetly. 'I think you're really going to like these two!'

Soon the surgery door opened again and Mr Parker Smythe backed awkwardly in. He carried a bulky, square shape. Imogen had to hold the door for him to get through.

'Careful!' Mrs Parker Smythe warned from behind in her high, silvery voice. 'That's a good girl, Immi! Let Daddy come right through. Now try not to get too excited, or you'll upset the poor baby rabbits!'

Mandy gasped and held on to the counter for

support. James stared at her wide-eyed. 'Did she say baby rabbits?' Mandy repeated.

'What did I tell you?' Jean beamed at them. 'I knew you'd both gone mad on rabbits lately. You and John Hardy!'

Mr Parker Smythe put the hutch down gently on the shiny floor. Slowly, a brown shiny nose appeared through the hole in the wooden partition of the hutch. Then two brown ears, two bright, shining eyes. One rabbit hopped into view. A second identical one came after.

'Button!' Mandy cried.

'Barney!' James followed her across and they both crouched down by the wire mesh at the front of the hutch.

The two baby rabbits sniffed at their new surroundings and stared out wide-eyed. An ear twitched, a paw scuffed in the straw. They sniffed the disinfected air.

'Like them?' Mr Parker Smythe inquired. He stood back, hands in pockets.

Slowly Mandy stood up and stared at Imogen.

'It was love at first sight as far as Immi was concerned,' he explained. 'Now we can hardly drag her out of the garden to go to bed at night, with these two to look after!'

Mandy took a deep breath. They'd found what they were looking for. But now it was going to take all her tact and skill to get Button and Barney safely back to John Hardy!

Nine

'Hello, Imogen.' Mrs Hope put her head round the treatment room door. 'We're all ready for Button and Barney now. Let's take a look at them, shall we?' She smiled at Mandy. 'Why not get your white coat and come and give me a hand?' she suggested. 'Simon's caught up next door with a spaniel with an injured paw.'

Mandy's head was spinning, but she did as she was told. With clumsy fingers she fastened the buttons on her white lab coat and followed Mr Parker Smythe and the rabbits into the treatment room.

'Can Immi come too?' Mrs Parker Smythe

pleaded from outside. 'She promises not to be a nuisance!'

'Of course she can. Come in, Imogen,' Mrs Hope said. 'Just close the door nice and tight, so the rabbits can't hop about and escape. That's right. Now, let's see what we have here!' Gently she lifted Button out of the hutch.

Emily Hope's calm voice had a soothing effect. Mandy told herself to think straight. Perhaps there was a way of sorting this out. OK, so Imogen Parker wasn't the kindest and most generous person she'd ever met. She probably didn't even know what the word sharing meant. But there had to be a first time for everything! She watched as her mother handed Button over to his new owner and bent forward to take Barney from the hutch.

'I'm glad you've brought them along, Mr Parker Smythe.' Mrs Hope inspected Barney's ears, then gently massaged his bottom jaw to open his mouth. She peered inside. 'Rabbits can easily fall ill with small infections, especially of the eye and ear. They need vaccinations, to be repeated every twelve months or so. The sooner we protect them against disease, the better.'

Barney nestled comfortably in the crook of her arm while she ran her fingertips over his abdomen and chest. She smiled. 'But he's certainly a healthy little chap at the moment!' She gave her verdict and handed him to Mandy. Then she began her examination of Button.

Mandy cradled the lightweight ball of warm fur, holding Barney close against her chest. His round, pretty face stared up at her, ears flat, nose twitching. Her mother began to prepare a syringe, while Imogen took Button and stroked him, laying her cheek against the soft brown fur of his back.

'Shh, Button. No one's going to hurt you! Shh!' Imogen half sang in the rabbit's ear. Her lips were parted in a soft, round shape. She crooned and

stroked her precious pet. Mr Parker Smythe stood back, watching his daughter with quiet satisfaction.

Even Mandy had to admit that this was a new girl who stood before her. The spiteful, selfish child who stamped her feet and swung moodily on her garden swing was gone. In her place was a sweet, loving seven-year-old.

Oh dear! Mandy frowned. How could she spoil Imogen's day by suggesting that she give Button and Barney back to John Hardy? She couldn't just say that they really belonged to John because he was the one who'd bought them in the first place! This was much more difficult than she'd expected.

'Hush, Button, there, there! That didn't hurt too much, did it?' Imogen scooped the rabbit back off the table as soon as Mrs Hope had finished the injection. The tiny creature quivered at the sharp needle, but he soon calmed down under Imogen's gentle touch.

Next it was Barney's turn. Imogen insisted on being the one to hold him too, while Mrs Hope went to work once more. So Mandy took Button from her and put him back in his hutch. He settled quietly into the clean straw.

'It looks like you made a good choice,' Emily

Hope said to Mr Parker Smythe. 'I know that you've been looking around for a pet for Imogen for quite some time. You must be very pleased to have found just the right ones!' She stood back, peeling off her surgical gloves.

'Oh, it's marvellous,' he agreed. 'You should have seen Imogen's face when we gave them to her. It was a picture!'

Oh dear! Mandy took a deep breath. *Why can't life be more simple?* She helped Imogen to fasten the front catch on the hutch. Button and Barney were both snuggled into the straw. This was a situation she hadn't expected to face; either Imogen or John was bound to end up broken-hearted.

'There *is* one thing, though.' Mr Parker Smythe drew Mrs Hope to one side. 'As you know, we've thought and thought about pets for Immi, and often we've decided that we're just too busy to fit them in. You know, I work away quite a lot, and we have a house in Tuscany which we like to visit whenever we can. We'd be there right now, except that I have some business I need to clear up.'

Mrs Hope nodded. She put her head thought-fully to one side, pushed back a wisp of red hair and listened hard.

'Anyway, we took the plunge with these two rabbits, and we're all thrilled to bits with them both. But I promised my wife that I'd ask you what you thought we might do with them during the holidays. You see, it's quite a problem for us, having pets and travelling about so much.'

If Mandy had been a rabbit, her ears would have shot up. As it was, she sprang upright and stared across the room at the grown-ups. *Maybe . . . just maybe!*

'You want a reliable bunny-sitter?' Mrs Hope considered the problem. 'For school holidays? I take it that Imogen doesn't want to part with them during term-time, when she's at home?'

'Oh, no!' Imogen gasped. 'And I won't ever go on holiday ever again, if it means leaving them all alone, with no one to look after them properly!' She was stung to tears at the prospect.

'Immi!' Her father smiled uncomfortably. 'You know we've already discussed this! You promised not to make a fuss, remember?' He shrugged at Mrs Hope.

'No, no, she's quite right. You do need a good, firm arrangement. So many people just go off and leave their pets without proper food and water, let alone exercise. You simply wouldn't believe it!' She paused, arms crossed, wondering what was the answer. 'But I'm afraid we don't do a boarding service here at Animal Ark. We don't have the space, you see. But we could put up a notice for you. There's a notice-board out in the waiting-room. Perhaps that would lead to something?'

'No need!' Mandy stepped forward. She clasped her hands in front of her to stop them trembling. 'I think I've got the answer!'

There was no such thing as magic in the real world, she knew. But this had just come close. And in an instant, she was about to make one sad boy happy!

Everyone at Animal Ark agreed that it was a brilliant idea. Mandy burst out into reception to tell James. 'Fantastic!' he gasped, rocking back on to his heels. Jean smiled broadly from behind her desk. Even Mrs Parker Smythe looked relieved. 'Are you sure that's all right, Immi? John Hardy does sound like just the right person to look after your rabbits while we're away! And since you haven't decided on names, yet, I think Button and Barney sound perfect.'

Imogen nodded. 'I suppose so.' She cocked her head sideways, looking serious and grown-up. 'And I do like the names.'

Now Mandy was all action. 'Now, let me ring John's dad to see what he thinks,' she said. 'If he says yes, why don't you and Button and Barney come and check to see whether you think the Fox and Goose is OK?'

Imogen thought about it. She peered wistfully into the hutch. 'OK,' she said slowly, her frown easing. 'If you're sure it'll be all right, Mandy.'

'More than all right! John loves rabbits, and he knows everything about them. He'll take really good care of them, don't you worry!'

'When would he have them?'

'Just whenever you have to go away, during the holidays.'

'Half-term,' Mrs Parker Smythe said. 'That would be the first time we'd have to leave them.'

'And maybe tonight?' Mandy asked. 'Just so Button and Barney can get used to John before he goes back to school. Then they won't be so nervous when they go there at half-term.'

'Good idea.' Mr Parker Smythe had relaxed. The crisis was over. He wanted another quick word about the rabbits with Mrs Hope before they left.

Meanwhile, Mandy reached for the phone to explain everything to the Hardys.

'I'm sorry, Julian's not in,' Sara said. 'And John's up at High Cross, of course!' She had listened carefully to the news. 'But I think it's an absolutely great answer to the problem. I tell you what, let's keep it a secret from John. You bring the rabbits over here for this trial run, and I'll find somewhere to hide them for when he comes in. I just want to see his face when he discovers them. It'll make his day! Well, it'll change his life, as a matter of fact. Thank you so much, Mandy!'

The phone clicked and Mandy went ahead, making sure that Imogen was happy with all their plans. 'Thanks for letting John have Button and Barney for tonight,' she told her when they had reached the Fox and Goose. 'I know it's hard for you to let them go.'

'Yes, but they will be all right, won't they?' Imogen was trailing after her father across the pub carpark. She watched anxiously as he took the hutch in through the back garden.

'Come in, I'll show you,' Mandy promised. 'Sara said she'd find just the right hiding-place for them; somewhere secret where John won't spot them when he first comes in. Come on, let's go and see!'

They went upstairs, along the crooked corridor, into John's room.

James and Mandy went in ahead of Imogen, who hung back. Then she crept in behind them and stared round at the walls covered in photos and sketches; dozens of rabbits, hundreds of rabbits; close-ups, long distance, at play or feeding. 'Where are they?' she whispered. 'Where's Button and Barney?'

'In here!' Mr Parker Smythe called out. 'Through this door. What do you say to this, Immi? Bunnies in the bathroom!'

He held the door open wide and pointed to the two little brown rabbits peering curiously round the white tiled space. 'Satisfied? Now let's say goodbye for now and leave Mandy and James to settle them down. We can come back and collect them early tomorrow. That's a good girl; I'm very proud of you.' He took her by the hand.

Imogen sniffed. Her mouth puckered. She bent down close to the hutch. 'Goodbye, Button! Goodbye, Barney! See you tomorrow!' She whispered.

By teatime, Mandy and James could hardly bear

to wait any longer. They were certain that John would stay up at High Cross until dusk; another two or three hours of unbroken suspense.

'Let's go on up there!' James suggested. 'We could persuade him to come down early.'

'No way!' Mandy bit her lip. 'He won't come until the very last rabbit's disappeared down its burrow. It's his final day. Wild horses wouldn't drag him away!'

'OK. Anyway, he'd probably suspect something.' James sat down again on the grass in the pub garden. It was a clear evening, with a tint of pink in the sky. Dusk tonight would be long and late.

'No, we just have to wait.' Mandy sat cross-legged under the apple tree. White blossom drifted on to the grass. Glasses clinked and customers chatted in the bar. 'Anyway, Button and Barney are both asleep.'

'Well, they've had a busy day.' James leaned back on his elbows.

Soon Sara brought out a tray of lemonade and crisps. 'Julian's just got back from town,' she told them.

'And?' Mandy got to her feet. 'What's he say?' Surely Mr Hardy wouldn't object to the new plan; not after all this!

'Come here!' Sara waggled her finger at them.

They crept indoors and up the stairs. Inside John's room, Mr Hardy was busy fixing big white display boards on to steel frames. He wanted to arrange his son's sketches and photos into an artistic display before John came home. He turned quickly and saw them peering in.

They lent a hand, pinning up the pictures, making sure they were straight. But it still wasn't even dusk by the time they finished. Mandy glanced at her watch, then at James.

Mr Hardy stood back to judge the effect of their work. 'Do you think he'll like it?' he whispered. 'It's a big surprise!'

Mandy and James nodded. 'It's not the only one!' James added.

'Thanks for your help,' Mr Hardy whispered. 'Now why don't you two scoot up to High Cross and meet up with that son of mine. Tell him I said it was time he got himself back home. But don't let on. I want everything to stay a complete surprise!'

Ten

John sat on his low rock by the nursery warren.
His sketchbook lay across his knees. His camera
still had its lens cap fixed firmly in place. He sat
in the fading light. All around, the rough grassland
dipped and rose; hazy green, alive with rabbits.

'Shh!' Lydia warned. She came out of the house
to walk with Mandy and James across to the far
pasture. They were ankle-deep in grass and
buttercups. 'I've had my eye on him all day, poor
little mite. It breaks my heart to see a boy so alone.'

'Let's wait until the rabbits have gone in before
we interrupt him,' James whispered. They came
to a stop by the low wall and stood watching.

Mandy longed to run across and send the
rabbits scattering across the hillside. She wanted
to run up to John and give him the good news.
But she kept her promise to his dad. They studied
the mist rising slowly from the valley. It crept
amongst the trees, over the patchwork fields. 'Has
there been any more trouble with Dean and
Steve?' she asked Lydia.

Lydia gave a wicked little smile. 'Not a squeak.
Sam Western, their boss, came to see me though.
According to him, the old land dispute was settled
in favour of Upper Welford Hall. In other words,
John over there *is* sitting on common land!'

'But?' James prompted.

'But I didn't let him get away with that, let me
tell you!' She laughed. 'I told him to go and check
his facts with the Land Registry. Meanwhile, he'd
better keep Dennis Saville and his lads off *my*
land!'

Mandy grinned. 'Phew!' Mr Western was known
as a loud-mouth and a bully. He wasn't popular,
but he did have friends in high places.

'Don't worry.' Lydia stood, hands in pockets,
collar turned up. 'That man's a stickler for laws
and lawyers himself. He won't dare send men out
here with their guns while there's a question mark

over who owns the land. When our friend John comes back home in a month or two, I guarantee he'll still be able to come up to this warren and find it just as it is now. Peace and quiet; that's what we like.' She breathed in deeply and threw her shoulders back. 'Peace and quiet!'

At last the light faded from the hill. The mist rose and the rabbits went to ground. John sat on in the damp twilight.

Mandy glanced uncertainly at Lydia.

'Go on, you two. It's time for you all to go home. You go and fetch him now.' She smiled at them both and said goodbye. 'Take care of that young man for me, and tell him there's a cup of tea for him at High Cross any time he cares to drop in!' She wandered off across her field, back to the house.

John looked up at Mandy and James as they trudged through the wet grass towards the rock. He uncrossed his legs and tucked his sketchbook under one arm. 'Hi,' he said in a flat voice. 'It's OK, I've finished here. I was just about to come down.'

'Your dad says you have to come home,' James told him. 'They say you've been up here all day.'

'Well, they don't have to worry about that now,

do they? After tomorrow I'll be gone, and they'll be alone together, just those two!'

'Oh, I don't think they want to get rid of you,' Mandy put in. 'In fact, I'm sure they don't. They've been really worried about you since—'

'Never mind!' John jerked to his feet. 'Anyway, it was a waste of time you two dragging yourselves all the way up here. I was on my way without needing to be told!'

Mandy nodded and kept her head down. John was in no mood to be friendly. They walked silently across the fields, making their way through the mist, guided by fence-posts and trees, until they reached the lane leading down into the village.

'It'll be dark before we get back,' James warned. 'Or just about, at any rate.'

Mandy and he chatted on about Lydia's goats, about school on Monday; homework they hadn't done and friends they would see. John walked in silence, locked away, lost in his own thoughts.

He didn't even notice when they walked on past the crossroads with him, instead of turning off to their own houses. He walked on through the village, head down, his dark figure striding two or three steps ahead. James and Mandy jogged the final stretch to catch him up. They entered the pub garden together.

They were greeted by the buzz of customers drinking in the bar. It sounded cosy and warm. But John went straight upstairs, not knowing or not caring that the other two still followed. His door stood open. He went in, unzipped his jacket and flung it on the bed with his sketchbook and camera.

'Surprise!' Mr Hardy stood with one arm round Sara's shoulder. He revealed the new gallery of John's work, waiting for a reaction.

John hesitated and blinked.

'What do you think?' His father came forward. 'Do you like it?'

'Yes, thanks, Dad, it's great.' John attempted a smile, but his voice gave him away. 'But you shouldn't have gone to all this trouble.'

'No trouble,' Mr Hardy said uneasily. 'Don't you think they look really professional? We'll have to talk about you taking it up as a job when you leave school.'

John shrugged. 'I don't know.' His own rabbits stared silently back at him from every angle.

Then Sara came forward and took him by the hand. 'Surprise number two,' she said gently. She

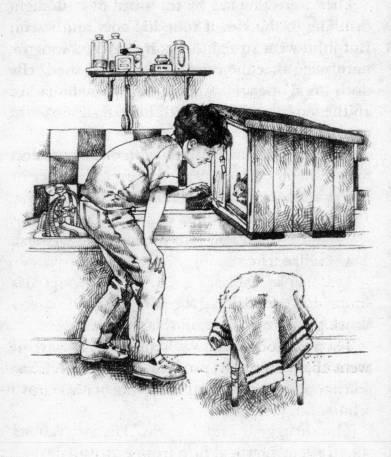

led him through to the bathroom.

Button and Barney had done what all rabbits do; they'd woken up to feed and play as night fell. They bobbed and hopped about inside their hutch, which rested on two planks of wood, carefully placed across the width of the white bath. As John approached, they hopped forward to the wire mesh, and poked out their noses in greeting.

'Carrot?' Sara offered. She handed two pieces to him.

He took them, too stunned to say anything. Button and Barney curled back their lips to show their long front teeth. They waited for their treat.

Mandy watched as John's blank face broke into a smile. The rabbits set to and nibbled. He crouched there with all the patience in the world, waiting until every scrap of carrot was gone.

Then he stood back. Without saying a word, he went up, put his arms round his father's neck and buried his face in the soft blue wool of Mr Hardy's best golfing sweater.

That evening they celebrated. John dashed downstairs to consult Ernie Bell about building a wire run for Button and Barney. 'Can it run the length of the whole garden, so they have lots of space to come out and feed?' he wanted to know.

Ernie sipped his beer. He winked at Mandy. 'Oh, aye, I reckon it can.'

'And will it be strong enough to keep them in, so they can't escape?'

'Aye. I'll make it just like the run I made for my Sammy, only not so high. Sammy, being as he's a squirrel, likes to climb a bit, see.'

John nodded. 'Rabbits like to dig. They won't be able to dig their way out, will they?'

'No problem. I'll put a good barrier along each edge, well dug in. Matter of fact, I've already promised one to the Parker Smythes up at Beacon House. It looks like I'm going to have my work cut out.'

John backed off, satisfied. Button and Barney were going to live in the lap of luxury in both their houses.

Walter Pickard, sitting across the table, tutted. 'I don't know, young man. You'll be wanting one of them Jacuzzi things for them before long!'

'Rabbits don't like water!' John laughed.

'Aye well, then, it'll be an 'utch with a patio and a sun umbrella!'

Mandy got up to go. 'James's dad has just arrived to give us a lift,' she told John.

'Yes, and I've got to go and pack,' he said. 'And check up on Button and Barney, of course.'

'Don't worry, they'll be OK,' she grinned. 'They're probably fast asleep again.'

'Thanks to you,' he nodded. He breathed a deep, happy sigh. 'I'll be back in six weeks. Ernie says the run will be ready by then.' He looked away, scratched his ear and gave a dry cough. He was blushing as he turned back to her. 'Er, Mandy . . .'

'What?' She saw Mr Hunter and James hovering by the door. 'Look, John, I've got to go!'

'Will you write to me?' he asked in a rush. 'Tell me how Button and Barney are getting along up at Beacon House. I mean, it's OK if you don't want to; you don't have to!'

'Of course I will!' she promised. A smile swept across her face. 'Any excuse to go and visit those bunnies!'

'Rabbits!' he said sternly. 'Er, Mandy, do you think you could manage to write to me, say, once a week?' he stammered.

'Twice!' she promised again. 'Three times! Whenever there's any news!'

'Oh, thanks!' John had turned crimson to the roots of his hair. 'Now I know it's not going to be half as bad!'

As it happened, John wrote first. A letter fell on the mat at Animal Ark on the Tuesday of the following week. Mandy was still in her pyjamas, with slippers wet from going out across the dewy grass to feed her own rabbits. She yawned as she opened the scribbled note:

Dear Mandy,

*   How are Button and Barney? Have they settled in at Beacon House? Tell Imogen not to feed them too much lettuce; it's too rich for them to have every day. I got an A++ for my project. Sorry if that sounds like boasting. I hope James is OK.*

*   Love, John*
P.S. Don't forget to write back soon about Button and Barney.

She wrote:
Dear John,

*   Button and Barney are fine. Ernie's started to build the run at Beacon House. But guess what? We all made a mistake. We thought Button and*

Barney were both boy rabbits. All right then, male rabbits. But Mum says we were wrong. Barney's a male, but Button's a female! Mum says she's absolutely sure. There's no doubt about it.

Mr Parker Smythe wanted to book Button into Animal Ark for her operation. But Imogen wants them to have one litter of babies first. (Sorry, kittens!) Her mum and dad said yes. So guess what again? Button and Barney could have babies soon! Isn't that great? Just think – baby Buttons and Barneys! What could be better?

    Love, Mandy

He wrote back a one-line letter:

Dear Mandy,

    Great news. OK, so I guess I don't know every-thing about rabbits!

      Love, John.

ANIMAL ARK AS SEEN ON TV
LUCY DANIELS

☐	70908 1	KITTENS IN THE KITCHEN	£3.50
☐	70911 1	PONY IN THE PORCH	£3.50
☐	70912 X	PUPPIES IN THE PANTRY	£3.50
☐	70913 8	GOAT IN THE GARDEN	£3.50
☐	71349 6	HEDGEHOGS IN THE HALL	£3.50
☐	70909 X	BADGER IN THE BASEMENT	£3.50
☐	71345 3	PIGLET IN A PLAYPEN	£3.50
☐	70914 6	BUNNIES IN THE BATHROOM	£3.50
☐	71346 1	DONKEY ON THE DOORSTEP	£3.50
☐	70910 3	HAMSTER IN A HAMPER	£3.50
☐	71350 X	GOOSE ON THE LOOSE	£3.50
☐	71347 X	CALF IN THE COTTAGE	£3.50
☐	71348 8	GUINEA PIG IN THE GARBAGE	£3.50

All Hodder Children's books are available at your local bookshop or newsagent, or can be ordered direct from the publisher. Just tick the titles you want and fill in the form below. Prices and availability subject to change without notice.

Hodder Children's Books, Cash Sales Department, Bookpoint, 39 Milton Park, Abingdon, OXON, OX14 4TD, UK. If you have a credit card you may order by telephone – 01235 831700.

Please enclose a cheque or postal order made payable to Bookpoint Ltd to the value of the cover price and allow the following for postage and packing:
UK & BFPO – £1.00 for the first book, 50p for the second book, and 30p for each additional book ordered up to a maximum charge of £3.00.
OVERSEAS & EIRE – £2.00 for the first book, £1.00 for the second book, and 50p for each additional book.

Name ....

Address ....

....

....

If you would prefer to pay by credit card, please complete:
Please debit my Visa / Access / Diner's Card / American Express (delete as applicable) card no:

Signature ....

Expiry Date ....